Swiss Cheese and Sibling Rivalry

Judy Volhart

Open Books

Published by Open Books

Copyright © 2019 by Judy Volhart

ISBN-13: 978-1948598163

Dedication

On September 21, 2018, shortly after 5pm, an EF3 tornado swept through the town of Dunrobin, a suburb of Ottawa, Ontario. The fictional town of Robin in the Whine & Cheese series was based loosely on this small town. Furthermore, the bistro in the series was inspired by a restaurant called the Heart and Soul. While the restaurant is still standing, a gift shop, located maybe 40 or 50 feet away on the same property, was obliterated by the ghastly winds ranging from 136 to 165 miles per hour. Only sad piles of rubble remain, a family business destroyed in minutes—nay, seconds—that felt like an eternity to anyone who experienced the storm.

The mini mall, not quite directly across the street, sustained considerable damage but was still standing. Right behind it, three houses were destroyed. Directly across the field from there, Amalia Kis's parents' home was damaged, but was otherwise left structurally sound. In reality, this is the house that I owned and lived in for over a decade, and the house my son still lives in with his dad. Gracie, my son's girlfriend, was home at the time, while my son was travelling from the complete opposite end of Ottawa after work, trying to get home, watching the tornado, in horror, from a distance.

Many homes in the area were completely annihilated and many more sustained considerable damage. In my son Kyle's words, "Everything's fucked. Just madness here." There were no graceful words to describe the situation.

The storm went on to damage many more homes across the river, on the Quebec side, and another three or four tornados reportedly cropped up in the Ottawa and surrounding areas. As I write this, only a week has passed, so the pain and horror is still fresh for many. Relief efforts are ongoing as people continue the clean-up and rebuilding process. Getting into Dunrobin is difficult as security guards refuse entry to anyone without a permission slip. Tempers flare, the stress for the residents builds.

Ominous clouds and rain persisted during the week, triggering episodes of Post Traumatic Stress Disorder. I had gone into Ottawa myself mid-week for my immunotherapy injection and watched nervously as angry clouds formed over the city. Luckily, no tornado warnings were issued, and after a brief rain, the clouds moved along and the sun shone.

I debated rewriting the ending of this book to incorporate these events, but the debate lasted all of one minute. I couldn't do it; it was just too close to home. It was home, at one time. Though I'm safely tucked away in Brockville, about 45-50 minutes away from the western part of Ottawa, my heart goes out to the city that I lived in for 26 years. The majority of my friends and family still live in the area, all of my doctors are there: a large part of my life still involves this city. Perhaps, subconsciously, it is for this reason that even when writing this book, I couldn't bear to have Amalia cut her ties completely from the town, the bistro and her friends.

It will always be home.

Cheers, my friends.

Chapter One

I drooled over the variety of cheeses set out before me at the deli. How could I possibly decide which ones to buy? I wanted it all.

Always worried about being able to pay my mortgage, I'd started hosting wine and cheese tasting events at the Whine and Cheese bistro that I owned in the town of Robin, just on the outskirts of Ottawa. Tonight's theme was Switzerland, and the shop owner had gathered a variety of Swiss cheeses for me to choose from. After much hemming and hawing, I finally walked out with some Emmental (which is usually the actual cheese that we call "Swiss"), it's close cousin, Gruyère, Appenzeller and some Raclette.

Naturally, I had visited the deli meats section as well and was already mentally envisioning my feast when a hard bump against my shoulder sent my purchases sprawling across the parking lot.

"Hans!" I spit his name and bared my teeth. Pretty Boy looked equally surprised to see me. He usually swung by my bistro every so often just to torment me with his presence, but I had not seen him since his last visit when he had blubbered something about "why had I left him?" I shuddered in disgust at the memory.

I'd lived with Hans for six years before finding the courage to end the relationship. He wasn't a bad person, just selfish and lazy. I tossed my cinnamon-coloured hair out of my eyes as I scooped my packages back into my bag. He made no effort to help. In fact, by the time I turned to glare at him, his overly long legs had carried him away. I glared anyway.

The twenty-minute drive home was agonizing. I had placed the food in the back seat, where I knew I couldn't reach it, but I could still smell the smoked Hungarian sausage and the garlic salami. After what seemed like forever, I pulled into my parking lot and was surprised to see Officer Lynette sitting on my front porch.

My blood curdled. What now? Although she was friendly enough, I doubted that this was a social call.

I put both left feet forward as I exited my vehicle and promptly fell on my face. Yes, this was typical of me. Embarrassed, I quickly gathered my purchases and approached her, trying to gauge her mood. A crease wrinkled her brow. Nope, this couldn't be good.

"Hello, Lynette, how are you?" I asked hesitantly.

"What's more important is how you are," she replied, peering at me closely. I suddenly felt guilty, as though I was being accused of a crime, likely because of my Catholic upbringing and her cop stare that looked deep into the mind, searching for secrets.

"I think I'm good. Am I?"

"I don't think so," she answered in all seriousness. "There was a break-in here." She watched closely for my reaction as tears immediately flooded my eyes. I didn't know what to say and had I known, I wouldn't have been able to choke it out anyway. I sat on a patio chair next to her and took a few dozen calming breaths, thankful for the yoga classes I had recently taken. "Is anything damaged?" I finally squeaked out.

"Not that I could tell. Your brother seems quite shaken though."

"Stephen? What's he doing here?"

"You weren't expecting him?" She looked even closer at me as I wiped the tears off my face and returned her scrutinizing look with one of confusion.

"No, I wasn't. I haven't heard from him in weeks, in fact, although that's not unusual. We have a rather hot and cold relationship." Her cop brows rose inquisitively.

"Well, it seems he came by to surprise you, but was instead surprised by a door wide open and the place ransacked. Any clue as to what someone might have been after?"

I was stumped. I had nothing of any value. As she led me inside, my confusion compounded. The place was untouched. "Is this a joke? Everything seems fine to me."

"Everything's fine down here in the bistro," she said. "It's your apartment upstairs that has been ransacked." I suddenly felt ill and sank onto one of the cozy couches in the bistro. I had assumed it was the bistro that had been violated, not my personal space. I followed her up the inner stairway to my home above the bistro. As usual, my beautiful and friendly cat, Hummer, wound himself around my ankles. Then he sat and blinked with distaste at my brother.

Stephen was sitting on the couch, still being questioned by another officer that I was relieved to see was not Officer Sean, Lynette's usual partner and my best friend Nicole's ex. He recounted his story, likely for the third or fourth time.

"I thought I'd surprise my sister with a visit. When I got here, the back door was wide open, as was the door to her place. There were no other cars in the parking lot and no one was here. That's all I know." His hands fidgeted with his silvery-black goatee. I noted that he looked far more grey than when I'd last seen him several months ago, when he'd helped my parents move from Montreal to just a few blocks away from me.

"Please look around and tell me if anything appears to be missing," Lynette instructed me.

I glanced around quickly. "Nope, nothing's missing." She looked at me skeptically. "I have nothing of value. The TV is still here, that's really the only thing worth taking." She insisted I take a closer look.

I inspected the kitchen, small pantry, bathroom, living/dining room and the two small bedrooms that made up my living quarters. While the place had obviously been rummaged through, nothing seemed to be missing because, as mentioned, I had nothing of real value. I wasn't sure if I was upset because someone had violated my personal space, or because I suddenly realized that, at the age of thirty-one, I had nothing worth stealing.

The police officers soon left, leaving Stephen and me alone.

"Nice moustache," he joked feebly, his usual loving banter.

"Screw you," I retorted, in no mood for him. I stopped myself from stroking my upper lip to ensure he wasn't serious. I knew damn well I didn't have a moustache. I must have checked it over a hundred times in my youth as a result of his merciless teasing. "Why are you here?"

"I thought I'd visit my favourite sister." Half-sister, and only one, I mentally corrected. We shared the same *alien* mother.

And speaking of which, as though I had just conjured them out of thin air, the *aliens* appeared in the still-open doorway.

"*Bazd meg,* Amalia!" My dad's mouth was agape as he inspected my upside-down home while swearing in Hungarian.

I fondly referred to my parents as aliens since they were so different from me, so Non-Canadian, stuck in 1960s Hungary. My mother spoke very broken English and no French. While my dad could muddle through quite effectively in English, he also did his fair share of butchering it. Both had been in Canada for longer than I was alive, so I failed to understand why they could not master the languages.

My mother's face brightened once she realized that Stephen was with me and she rushed to give him kisses. As usual, I was scolded while he basked in motherly love. I rolled my eyes, my pseudo-aneurism pulsing above my left eye.

"I needed a break from my two jobs so I thought I'd visit. When I got here, the place had been broken into. What have you gotten yourself into this time, Mali?" He loved throwing me under the proverbial bus any chance he got.

"Why are you working two jobs?" I switched the focus to him and he squirmed uncomfortably.

"Just trying to make ends meet." My mother didn't understand this English expression so I translated for her as we all switched to speaking Hungarian.

"You work so hard!" She immediately began rummaging through her purse for her wallet. Stephen had no qualms about accepting handouts and quickly tucked the hundred-dollar bill into his back pocket. I, on the other hand, would sooner become a hooker than accept money from my parents.

Realizing that I was in no mood for any of them, I politely suggested that they all return to my parents' place so I could put my home back in order. My dad looked a tad disappointed and I noted that subtle glean in his eyes, the same one I saw a few months ago when he was my trusty side-kick in helping solve the death of a woman who had collapsed in my parking lot.

Here's the thing: there's nothing spectacular about

me, and I like to lead a pretty quiet life. I was content to surround myself with wine, cheese, salami and a few close friends. But for some reason, people keep dying around me, and I always end up involved in solving the case. My only goal is to clear the name of the bistro so that my precious business doesn't go under, because then I'd have no way of paying my mortgage and other bills. I'd be out of both a business and a home, *and I didn't actually want to become a hooker because I was a bit on the shy side.*

Other than my gentle stubbornness and my clumsiness, I have no crime-solving skills. The last time around, my dad had actually prodded me into investigating and had tagged along a few times, much to my surprise, amusement, horror and utter respect.

Thankfully, there were no bodies here today, and no crimes to solve. It was a mystery as to why someone would break in, but the house was surrounded by a forest and set back from the road. Out here on the outskirts of Ottawa, break-ins weren't that uncommon. Other than the evil Mr. Leonardo down the street at the pizza joint, I had no enemies—at least none that I knew. And the only reason ol' Leo didn't like me was because I was his only competition in town.

I suddenly bolted upright when a tiny *mew* caught my ears. My stocky cat, Hummer, was several years old and did not *mew* feebly: he barked (I swear!). I went in search of the sound and discovered the cutest little black kitten sitting at the threshold of my still open door that led downstairs to the bistro.

Before I could bend down to pet him, Hummer came tearing into the room and swooped down on the little guy, pinning him to the ground with a roar. The kitten retaliated with a jab to the nose, prompting Hummer to look both surprised and offended. He turned to look at me and blinked in his special way.

"Hum, let go of the little guy!" I gently scooped the black fur ball safely into my arms and was rewarded with purrs. Hummer watched our every move, blinking his displeasure. "Traitor!" his look seemed to say.

"Where did you come from?" My answer was a nuzzle deep into my neck before it immediately fell asleep. Yup, unless someone stepped forward to look for a missing cat, he was now mine. I sat down gingerly, so as not to wake him while Hummer stood a few feet away, sniffing disdainfully in our direction. At one point, when the kitten stretched and repositioned himself, Hummer's tail grew puffy. I'm certain he kept one eye open at all times.

"You'll get used to him eventually, you old grump!" I chastised him gently. He gave me a look that again accused me of betraying him before he turned in a huff and walked away.

"Alright, little kittie, let's get you set up in the spare room, behind closed doors, so that you're not eaten by the big guy. I've got work to do!" I gave him a few kisses, filled a shallow cardboard box with newspaper and litter for him, gave him some food and water, and then closed the door to keep him safe. From what I could tell, it was a "him", but until I was sure no one was looking for the cat, I refused to name him.

In the kitchen, I gave Hummer a few extra treats as proof that I still loved him then I hurried down to the bistro.

I'd bought this building almost a year ago. It had already housed a restaurant on the main floor and living quarters above, so it was perfect for me. After selling a condo I owned in downtown Ottawa, I was lucky to have acquired this at a fairly good price since it had been vacant for a while. In a rut, I had quit my job at the insurance company that I had worked for and set out to pursue my dream of owning a bistro. More often than not, I wondered if I'd made the right choice. It had not been without its fair share of challenges.

Behind schedule, I rushed to prepare the platters of cheeses, breads and salamis for the evening's wine and cheese pairing event. It was no small task, since the final headcount was at eighteen and there were often last-minute guests as well who did not pre-book. I never turned them away and made sure to always prepare a couple of extra platters for this reason.

A wave of dizziness and nausea swept over me, making me realize that I had not eaten other than the taste-testing at the deli, now several hours ago. Not slowing, I shoved a piece of bread into my mouth. There was no time to dawdle.

Food ready and wine pairings selected, I tore around the dining room, frantically lighting the red and black candles on the tables. I caught a brief flash of headlights in the parking lot and knew that people were starting to arrive. A momentary feeling of panic bubbled up my esophagus as I unlocked the door and pasted a smile onto my face.

I am an introvert by nature, so why I decided to work with the public is beyond me. I was good at it, even though I preferred to remain behind the scene cooking or planning meals.

On cue, I turned on the charm, welcoming guests and checking them off the reservation list as they entered. I instructed them to sit where they liked as I made a final headcount: 21 today, a record turnout. But according to my list, one person was still missing.

"Stella?" I called, to locate the person who had reserved for two. She raised her hand meekly and I walked over to her table for two, which she occupied alone. "Will the other party be joining you, or shall we proceed?" I asked politely.

She blushed profusely, not liking attention to be focused on her. I placed her roughly at my age, with chin-length, bobbed, brown hair, brown eyes and pale skin.

"He should be here any minute," she apologized. I liked her immediately.

"No problem. We'll give him a little bit longer," I replied kindly. Hans used to be late all the time and it had driven me nuts, so I could easily relate to this lady. A few minutes later, I gave her a sympathetic glance but had to proceed as the crowd was growing hungry and a bit impatient.

Normally, serving this many people alone would

have been a nightmare. For a wine pairing event, however, I enlisted the help of the patrons by having them pass the bottles of wine around to each other and topping up their own glasses while I distributed the food. Each person had three glasses already waiting for them at the tables: one for red wine, one for white and the last for water to cleanse their palates. A half hour into the event, and two different wine, cheese and salami pairings later, we took a break. Poor Stella's date still had not arrived. Catching her eye, I gave her a smile.

I was about to stride toward her when a *clang* from the bistro's kitchen caught my ear. Darnit! The lock on the back door was still broken, so anyone could waltz inside. I made my way toward the noise and cautiously poked my nose into the kitchen, but all was in order. I slowly approached the rear of the house. The back entrance consisted of my office, and to this day, I could still visualize the body that had been hanging from the coat hooks by the door on the day that I had moved in. I shuddered at the thought, but pushed it aside. After all, that was a long time ago now.

I was suddenly grasped by hands around my waist and before I could shriek, lips clamped down on my own. Fear quickly turned to lust, then mild anger, as I leaped away, swatting at my assailant. "Nathan, you scared the crap out of me! What are you doing here?" He laughed heartily at my expense.

"Sorry, baby. I just couldn't wait to see you. It's been almost two weeks." Nathan was the love of my life, even though we'd only been dating a few months. In that short time, he had worked his way into my heart, proclaimed his love, then promptly moved two hours away to Kingston for a promotion.

He was a paramedic and had accepted a one-year contract as an emergency services team leader shortly after we met. What would happen after the year was up was anyone's guess, but in the meantime, I missed him like crazy. Every spare minute we had was spent commuting between the two cities to see each other. Although he'd asked me to move with him, I could not simply walk away from the bistro, especially not after such a short time knowing him.

"I wasn't expecting you until tomorrow. I'm in the middle of a wine tasting event," I gave him a lingering kiss then pushed myself away. "You're welcome to wait upstairs, but I have to get back to work." A final kiss and I returned to the dining room while he took the stairway up to my apartment.

I did a quick headcount, came up with 21, and was about to start when my senses began to tingle. Something wasn't quite right. I scanned the crowd again, trying to pinpoint the issue. My eyes landed on the table with the lady with the giant, flashy earrings and big, bushy, black hair. Her friend, her opposite, with demure pearl earrings and sleek, blonde hair, was not with her. Had I miscounted? I started over, stopping when I reached Stella, and then smiled. It looked like her date had finally arrived. She caught my eye, grinned in return, and just then he turned to face me.

My heart froze and my mouth gaped open. It was Officer Sean.

I mentally snarled his name–Nicole's, ex-boyfriend. Everything about that brief relationship had been wrong, but somehow she had fallen for him and had her heart broken. Out of loyalty to her, I glared at him, and he smiled at me.

Grimacing, I shifted my attention back to the flamboyant dark-haired lady and made my way to her table.

"Excuse me, but will your friend be returning?" I asked politely. Occasionally, people have to leave suddenly during these events due to baby-sitter issues or other matters.

A frown creased her brow. "I hope so. I'm starting to worry, to be honest. She went to the ladies' room about ten minutes ago. I texted her just now, to see if she was okay, but she hasn't responded. I know she had her phone with her. She's a lawyer and does not go anywhere without that phone. I was even teasing her because she had a wine glass in one hand and her phone in the other!" She joked feebly, but I could tell she was indeed worried.

"I'll see if everything's okay," I replied and hurried to the ladies' room. I knocked sharply on the door, impatient with the delay, and was surprised when it opened inward an inch.

"Hello?" I called out. I wasn't getting a good feeling about this. My ears strained, but no answer came from inside. I could see that it was dark inside, so

I snaked a hand through the door opening to turn on the light switch with a finger nail, repeating my hello, this time louder.

Past experience had also taught me to err on the side of caution. When I again received no answer, I whipped a used tissue from my pocket, wrapped it around my index finger, laughed at myself for probably over-reacting, and jabbed my covered finger at the door to push it open.

Then I saw the outstretched arm, and the limp body attached to it.

Better than Bushra's Chickpea Salad

Here's a story about a girl named Bushra. She's 16 and makes the best damn chickpea salad that she sells at her Syrian food stall at the local farmers market.

Well, second best. Smirk.

I didn't want to ask her for the recipe: a magician never reveals their tricks, right? So, I set out to re-create it myself. I have a pretty good palate and can pick out a lot of flavours. That, combined with some internet searches for somewhat similar recipes, gave me a good base to start with. I like to take what appeals to me from each recipe, combine it all together, and add my own "bit of this and a bit of that."

The end product was simply WOW. I've been eating this every day straight for over three weeks now and I'm excited to share the recipe. I recommend freezing about 1/3 cup of chickpeas to use in other recipes such as mixing in with rice or into a soup.

The Recipe

- 1 can chickpeas, well rinsed
- ¼ cup good quality, light-tasting olive oil
- 4 tablespoons lemon juice (the plastic lemon full of juice is fine)
- ½ of a large, firm tomato or 1 small tomato, diced
- 1 green onion (white and green part), diced

- 1 tablespoon chopped fresh cilantro (a must—don't skip this ingredient and it must be fresh, not dried)

- 1 teaspoon dried cumin (also a must)

- A few shakes from a jar of chili powder (about ¼ teaspoon, also a must!)

- A few shakes of dried dill weed

- 1 tablespoon chopped fresh parsley

- 1 teaspoon chopped fresh chives

- Salt and pepper to taste

- 2 tablespoons chunks of feta cheese (optional)

Combine all ingredients, mix and enjoy. Keeps well for a few days, if you don't eat it before then. To take it over the top, if you are familiar with a good quality feta cheese, it'll make the salad *to die* for.

Note that if you are adding cheese to this dish, it should be eaten the same day.

Don't be afraid to experiment. I often put a diced radish in this salad too. If you're not sure if something would go well, try it in a small bowl so that the whole salad isn't ruined if you don't like it.

Chapter Two

I froze, staring at the arm and what little of the body I could see through the half-open door. My tissue fell to the ground but I was hesitant to scoop it up–that would place me closer to the body. Of course, I could be jumping to conclusions. Maybe this woman had merely fainted and required medical attention. I'd been down this road too many times before though, and I wasn't taking any chances. My reflexes kicked in, telling me to treat this like a crime scene and just back away.

I glanced about furtively, noting no movement around me. The washrooms were around a bend, out of sight of the diners. I could hear muted conversations in the background. My mind spun. Call 911? Run upstairs to get Nathan? He was a paramedic, after all. Then, with a sudden clarity, my answer: Officer Sean. Never in a million years would I have thought that I'd be happy to see him.

I left the tissue behind and made my way to Sean's table. I murmured an apology to Stella for my interruption.

"Officer Sean," I said, with as much respect as I could muster, "may I have a word with you? It's urgent," I hastened to add.

His brows rose. "What have you gotten yourself into now?"

I merely cocked my head for him to follow me. I could feel the eyes of the dark-haired lady watching my every move, worried about her friend. I didn't dare meet her gaze.

Please let me be wrong, I whispered to myself, as I led Sean around the corner to the ladies' room.

"I saw the arm and backed away. I touched the light switch with a fingernail— nothing else. I used a tissue to push the door open—it was already ajar. *I don't know her!*" I felt the need to add this last bit in my defence, knowing it was the lady in question once I noted the demure pearl bracelet on her arm that matched the earrings I'd noticed earlier.

He did as I had done, glancing about before calling out, "Ma'am, are you okay? My name is Officer Sean. I'm coming in." He ordered me to step away, glared at me until I did, then pushed open the door.

I peered over his shoulder but immediately regretted it. Blood surrounded her head, with bits splattered about. I gagged as I backed away.

"Make sure that nobody leaves the building, but don't tell them anything," he snapped at me, his phone already at his ear to call for backup. "Do you know this woman?" He was checking for a pulse.

"No," I said. "But she's here with a friend."

"Go get her," he commanded. "But don't bring her back here. Just take her aside and have her ready for me."

I nodded and shuffled away, wondering what I would say to the friend and to the roomful of people.

Stella was the first to catch my eye, curious as to why I'd interrupted her date. I put a finger to my lips, indicating for her to remain quiet. I assumed she would know that Sean was a cop and seemed intelligent enough to realize that a crime had likely just taken place. Her widening eyes confirmed my suspicion. She reached for her wine glass and took a fortifying gulp, giving me the inspiration for my next steps.

"Everyone, can I have your attention please for a moment?" The room quieted and the guests looked at me expectantly. "Please forgive me, but something urgent has come up that requires my attention. In the meantime, I will distribute the next cheese plate and wine pairing for you to begin without me."

I continued speaking as I handed out bottles of red, pink and white Sibling Rivalry. "Please pour yourself a glass of whichever wine you prefer and then pass it around. This wine is from the St. Catherine's, Ontario region, fairly close to the Niagara Falls area. It is made by three brothers, hence the three varietals. There are three different grapes per each blend. The white is juicy with notes of citrus and apples. The pink is one that I associate with summertime, and the red reminds me of berries…"

My voice faded as I dashed into the kitchen for the cheese and salamis. I bustled back moments later, my arms loaded with plates, and I rushed to distribute them quickly. "Enjoy this lovely combination, and I will be back in a few minutes to tell you a little bit more about it."

I saved the last plate for the friend of the victim, pure brilliance on my part as this made our exchange look entirely innocent. "Can you please follow me out to the kitchen in a moment or two? I need to speak to you about your friend."

I retreated to the kitchen to wait for her, and she showed up a minute later, her face taut with anxiety. I led her to the back of the house and into my office.

"Have you found Merri?" Her voice trembled, sensing something was wrong.

"I think so. Did you happen to notice if she was wearing a pearl bracelet?"

She nodded her confirmation. "Please, tell me what's going on," she begged, her voice now barely above a whisper.

"I'm not sure," I replied honestly, since I really didn't have a clue. "She appears to have had an issue in the bathroom. Perhaps she fainted…" I didn't know what to say next. "Someone will be here shortly to give you an update."

As if on cue, Officer Sean appeared in the doorway. He cocked his chin toward the kitchen, indicating that I should leave, and I was only too happy to oblige. I did not want to be present when this woman was given the shocking news.

I returned to the dining area, prepared to continue

my speech about the wine and cheese pairing, but I was saved from doing so as the police backup and paramedics arrived. I directed the paramedics to the restroom and the police officers to the office where they would find Sean. The customers stared in confusion. Sean's partner, Officer Lynette, raised a brow at me as she passed.

"Long time, no see," she commented before entering the kitchen. I squared my shoulders and addressed the crowd.

"My apologies, ladies and gentleman, but it seems that there's been an incident this evening. The police will likely need everyone's name and statement. I'm sorry that I can't give you more information; that's really all that I know at this time." The room buzzed with excitement.

Officer Lynette returned at that moment and took over. At the same time, Nathan emerged from the kitchen area, having descended from my living quarters, no doubt having heard the ambulance and police car sirens. I went to join him and quickly explained what little I knew.

"I'll go see if the paramedics need a hand," he said before dashing away. Unsure of what to do, I followed and stopped at one of the couches near the front door, where I could see and hear almost everything that was going on. I sank onto the plush fake leather, barely resisting the urge to bang my head onto the table in front of me.

What now? Why here…again? I doubted that the

injury I had seen on that poor woman's head was an accident. My blood suddenly curdled: someone had done this while we were all just steps away. Was the killer still here?

Sean now joined Lynette. I listened to him instructing the patrons not to leave until an officer had taken statements. I snuck a peek at Stella. She was looking at Sean with adoration in her eyes. Funny, I would have thought that she'd be frightened by such a scene. My musings, however, were interrupted by the sight of Nathan, ghostly white and retching as he doubled over, clutching onto a wall for support.

Confused, I rushed to his side. Surely, being a paramedic, this was not how he reacted each time there was a body? My unspoken question was soon answered as he turned his anguished eyes in my direction.

"My sister…" he choked out, before retching again.

Chapter Three

"Your sister?" He had a sister? I didn't recall him ever mentioning one despite our many hours of conversation.

Lynette walked over to check out the commotion. "What's going on over here?" she asked roughly.

I patted Nathan on the back as he tried to regain his composure. When we didn't answer, her tone grew sterner.

"What are you two doing over here, anyway? You should be over there, with the others. That includes you, Amalia."

"That's my sister," Nathan squawked out again. "The bracelet she's wearing. It was our grandmother's. And she is wearing a top I had bought her years ago... when we still spoke to each other." Tears slid down his face and he swiped at them angrily.

"What was she doing here, Amalia?" His tone was sharp as he questioned me, taking me by surprise. As Lynette raised her brows, I envisioned them disappearing into her hairline.

"She was here with a friend, for the wine and cheese pairing event," I stammered, confused by his demeanour.

"That's all? Did she speak to you?" His tone was still flinty. Lynette observed our exchange wordlessly.

"Yes, I mean, no. Yes, that's all. No, she didn't speak to me. Nathan, why do you sound angry at me? She came here with a friend. The friend alerted me that she was concerned about Merri since she had been in the washroom for a long time and wasn't answering her cell phone, so I came to investigate and found her like…that. I've never seen her prior to today." I wasn't sure why I felt the need to add this small tidbit, but Nathan was obviously anxious; not just because she was dead, but because of her presence here.

"I'm sorry, Mali, I don't mean to take it out on you. I was just concerned that if she knew that we were dating, she might have been harassing you. She was disowned by our family years ago, so I was afraid she was trying to cause trouble. I would not have put it past her."

"This is all very interesting," Lynette finally spoke, her note pad now at the ready. "Amalia, I would like you join the rest of the people over there and wait for Sean to speak with you, while this gentleman and I continue this conversation." She steered Nathan away from me, and out of earshot.

I rejoined the rest of the crowd and sat down next to Stella. "Sorry about your date," I whispered tentatively.

She brushed my comment aside. "Oh, but isn't this exciting? He's so handsome, isn't he? Look at him, taking charge!" She gushed and I tried to look at Sean through her eyes but all I could see was the man who had broken Nicole's heart, then later turned nasty and stalked her. He had only stopped when my then-boyfriend, Matt, a private investigator and ex-cop, secretly video-taped him harassing her and then threatened to report him to the police chief, whom he knew personally.

I muttered politely. "How did the two of you meet, anyway?"

"Quite by accident, actually. You see, Lynette, his partner, is my sister. They were roommates for a while. Nothing happened between them, of course, since she's gay, otherwise I wouldn't have dreamed of dating him. She was furious when he asked me out." Stella giggled at the recollection. "Since they'd lived together, she knew him quite well and didn't have the best opinion of him, but then again, we seldom share the same opinions. You should have seen her trying to talk me out of dating him. She lives with me now, so I had to hear it day and night. Quite honestly, it just made me even more curious to meet up with him!" She laughed smugly.

So, this meek looking thing had a spark to her that I certainly hadn't expected. And I liked her, despite the fact that she was smitten with Sean. We spoke quietly for the next hour or so until Sean joined us. Having left us last to question, he took our statements and then announced that everyone was free to go. Everyone shuffled to the door, but only after collecting a voucher from me to come back for another wine and cheese pairing session free of charge. Once again, it seemed, the bistro's reputation would be at stake.

Lynette, Sean and Nathan joined Stella and me at our table. Nate had partially regained his composure but looked exhausted, while Stella's eyes danced with undisguised passion as she ogled Sean. Lynette caught my gaze and rolled her eyes, unamused. I couldn't help but grin, but then quickly wiped the smirk off my face as Sean looked at me in confusion.

"Amalia, why do things like this keep happening here?" he said gruffly.

"I wish I knew," I mumbled. "Nathan, when was the last time you saw your sister? Has she lived in Ottawa all this time?"

Sean's eyes snapped in his direction. Lynette had not yet had the chance to enlighten him of this development.

Seemingly deep in thought, he said, "It's been at least five years, perhaps longer. You see, she was a lawyer, and she was having a tough time with her spouse, as well as financial issues. Unfortunately, she swindled a few of her clients out of their money, charging their credit cards for services that she never rendered, before fleeing Ottawa and moving to British Columbia–at least that's what we thought. In her absence, we had to deal with her clients, who were trying to track her down. What a mess! We never even got an explanations or an apology from her. It was only through mutual friends that we even learned of her move. I don't know when she returned, or more importantly, why."

Sean scribbled furiously on his notepad. "This is

all very helpful. Perhaps her friend, with whom I spoke earlier, might be able to shed some light on all this. Lynette, did you get the information on the ex-spouse and former clients?"

She nodded her head. "Yes, Nathan and I spoke at length and he's told me everything he knows and whatever names he could remember. I'll begin tracking them down tomorrow."

"Will I be closed down again?" I asked quietly, already knowing the answer.

"For a day or two, yes. We'll try to keep it as brief as possible, Amalia," Lynette responded. She knew this was my livelihood, and being shut down for any length of time would be a disaster.

"Lynette, you don't suppose this is somehow linked to the break-in, do you?" I couldn't see why it would be, but suddenly remembered *that other mystery*.

"Since you didn't know Merri, I don't see how it could be, but we'll keep it in mind."

"What break-in?!" Nathan exclaimed. I hadn't had a chance to tell him about it: too lengthy to get into via text, and not wanting him to worry while he was out of town.

"Yes, someone broke into my living space and trashed it, yet, nothing seems to have been stolen. That's why you were able to get in through the back door; the lock is still broken."

"I don't like this one bit, Amalia. Maybe you should consider selling and moving in with me...." His voice trailed as he noticed my features harden.

"This is my baby, Nathan; I'm not giving up that easily." The tone of my voice left no room for argument and introduced Nathan to a side of me to which he'd not yet been exposed.

Sean, Stella and Lynette took their leave, while we locked up, tidied as best we could, and then dragged ourselves upstairs, falling into bed after an exhausting day.

The next day would prove to be just as challenging.

Chapter Four

We had slept in, both of us too drained to lift our heads before ten in the morning. I was the first to wake and made sure not to disturb Nathan who was snoring mercilessly. I studied him quietly for a few minutes before slipping out of bed. We had grown to know each other quite well in a relatively short amount of time, but this revelation about a sister that had never before been mentioned threw me for a loop. What else was he keeping from me?

Suddenly, I was quite relieved that I had not moved to Kingston with him. When he'd told me of his promotion, he had suggested that I join him there. I had declined, saying I could not leave my bistro after having only been open for such a short time, not to mention that our relationship was still extremely new.

What he didn't know, however, was that I later met with my ex-real estate agent, Janet Reno. As well as a representative of my mortgage bank. Both had confirmed what I already suspected: if I were to try to sell at this time, then I'd probably lose a significant amount of money as I had not yet built up enough equity. I silently thanked my lucky stars that I had not rushed head-long into anything.

I smirked to myself at the recollection of my meeting with Janet. It had provided the opportunity for me to express my displeasure that she had found my parents a home just minutes away from mine, when I had expressly requested that she only show them properties on the other side of town. She apologized sheepishly, admitting that my dad had insisted that she show him homes closer to mine or he'd switch agents.

In the kitchen, I gave Hummer a pet and refilled his food bowl before checking on the little kitten in the spare room. When I peeked inside the night before, it was sound asleep; now, it was raring to go, lunging playfully at my feet. Hummer had followed me into the room, and although his tail grew puffy, he showed some curiosity toward the small ball of fur.

I scooped up the kitten and then brought it down to Hummer's level so that they could sniff each other. After a few sniffs, and with his tail still puffy, Hummer backed out of the room. All in all, that had gone quite well, I thought. I felt it was safe enough to put the kitten down and allow it to follow me into the kitchen.

I had almost finished my first cup of coffee when Nathan shuffled into the room, looking as though the world were upon his shoulders. I gave him a long hug then quietly fixed him a mug of coffee. We drank in silence before he finally spoke.

"She swindled money out of us, too. Her own family! We only realized this later, of course. She'd come to each of us, asking to borrow money. Not a huge amount, but enough that it hurt the wallet. At that point, we'd all been close, so we thought nothing of it. Mind you, none of us knew that she'd asked each of us for money. It was only when we hadn't heard from her in a while, and that her clients started tracking us down, that we started comparing stories. How could she do this to her own family? Her husband was simply devastated." A few tears slid down his cheek, but lost in thought, he didn't seem to notice.

"I have to call everyone. I can't recall if Officer Sean said he'd be advising the family, but I think it is best if they hear it from me."

"Do you want me to go with you?" I stammered. I was hesitant to offer as I'd not yet met anyone in his family.

"I would like that Amalia, and thank you for offering, but it's best I do this alone. This certainly isn't the circumstance under which I wanted you to meet them. Oh, God!" His face fell as a thought struck him. "Since she was murdered here at your bistro, I wonder how the family will react to the news that you're my girlfriend." He looked completely crestfallen, and I reached out to hold his hand.

"We'll get through this. Maybe, for now, just don't mention that part..."

He shook his head. "They'll find out eventually. I think I had already mentioned having a date with the owner of the Whine and Cheese bistro so now that we're in a serious relationship, there's no sense hiding it. Why did she have to come here, of all places?"

"Do you know the friend that she was with?

"I didn't see her. Officer Sean had already spoken to her and had allowed her to leave by the time Lynette was done with me. What did she look like?"

"Big, bushy…" I started but was immediately cut off.

"Georgina! Yes, without a doubt. They've been best friends since primary school. I'll pay her a visit today."

"Do you mind if I tag along for that visit?" Like it or not, I was about to get involved and I wasn't going to miss my opportunity to question this lady. He nodded his approval, stated he'd be back for me later that afternoon, and then prepared to face his family.

Luckily, it was only Tuesday and the bistro would not normally open again until Thursday–if I was given permission by the police to re-open. In the meantime, I wanted to look around now that everything had been photographed, finger-printed and cleaned up from the night before. The crime scene tape was still up, of course, but I'd be sure not to disturb anything. I'd been through this a few times before and knew how to be cautious. Frankly, I was surprised that I'd been allowed to sleep on the premises. Perhaps it was just an oversight, but I wasn't about to question it.

I located the kitten in the bathroom and put it back in the spare room. It seemed to be getting along with Hummer (who still had a fat tail), but I thought it best to keep it in a separate room, just so that I had one less thing to worry about. Then I donned some vinyl gloves and headed down to the bistro.

I approached the client bathroom and slowed at the smell of cleaning fluids. I sat at a table nearby, trying to get used to the smell of disinfectants.

"Damnit!" I exclaimed out loud. In all the commotion, I had not taken a head count after I'd discovered Merri's body. I calmed slightly, remembering that I had done the count just before going in search of her and no one, except her, had been missing. But that didn't mean that someone had not slipped out afterwards.

I had not noticed much interaction between the customers, except when they passed around the wine, and no one that had spoken to her other than her friend. Nothing had seemed amiss.

"The best bet," I said aloud to myself, "is that someone simply came in the front door while we were taking our break. I would not have noticed, since I was busy, but it was certainly possible. Georgie insisted that she had had her phone in hand the entire time. Was she corresponding with someone?"

I went to the front door and pretended to enter as though I were a murderer. From there, one could see directly to the area where the client washrooms were located. That area, however, had not been fully lit during the tasting, since that had taken place closer to the kitchen in order to save me from having to run around too much. While the lights were lit at the front of the bistro, I had purposely kept them dim to prevent unnecessary wandering by the customers.

I slowly walked from the front door toward the washroom, carefully inspecting the ground in front of me, and noting nothing out of the ordinary. I retraced my steps, and then walked back to the washroom again, this time slowly looking to the left and right.

That was when I noticed the missing candle, and my stomach lurched.

Chapter Five

I closed my eyes, hung weakly onto the back of a chair, and breathed in the disgusting, antiseptic smell through my nose, willing my stomach to relax.

Each table had had a big, bulky, red or black candle on it to match the décor of the bistro. The one at this table was missing, and if my guess was correct, it was likely the murder weapon. I felt sickened that something of mine had been used in such a heinous crime, and it was all I could do not to lose the contents of my stomach. On shaky legs, I made my way back upstairs to my living quarters and made a call to Officer Lynette, leaving her a message to call me as soon as possible.

To my surprise, she showed up ten minutes later.

"I was down the street at Leonardo's when I got your message, so I thought I'd come by. You're not looking too good," she noted shrewdly.

"I never look good when Leonardo's name is mentioned," I joked feebly. Lynette knew of my feud with him—or rather his feud with me, since he'd made it well known that he despised my very existence.

She snickered at my lame joke. "I hope I'm not here for a rectal exam?" she joked back, noting the vinyl gloves I was still wearing. I looked down at the ground sheepishly.

"Well, I was looking around downstairs but didn't want to disturb anything."

She glared at me, but urged me to continue. "And I assume you found something that led to your phone call…"

I nodded. "Shall we go downstairs? I think you'll see for yourself?"

Once downstairs, we stood by the front door, looking into the room. "Look at all the tables. What's on each of them?" I prompted her.

"Candles?"

"Correct. Now, look at each table closely." She glanced about, and her eyes soon fell upon the table with the missing candle, the table that was the closest to the washrooms.

"Hot damn," she uttered softly. "Have you found it?"

"No. After I discovered the missing candle, I went back upstairs to call you immediately."

"Well, I hate to admit it, Amalia, but you've done well. Now that we know what we're looking for, why don't you go back upstairs while I check things out down here." It was less a question than an order, but I was only too happy to comply.

I couldn't help wondering how Nathan would react when he learned that not only had his sister been murdered at my bistro, but that the murder weapon was an object which I myself had placed upon each table. A soft sob escaped my throat and I quickly busied myself by making another pot of coffee. I was on my second cupful by the time Lynette joined me, gratefully pouring a mugful for herself then sitting on the couch next to me.

"I didn't find the candle, or anything else. But I agree that it is very likely the murder weapon. Those candles could very well have caused the type of injuries sustained by the victim. I'm going to have to take one so that we can compare it to the wounds–sorry."

I nodded, having fully expected the confiscation.

"Does anything unusual stand out in your mind about last night?" she asked me gently.

To my surprise, a bark of laughter escaped my lips. "I'm sorry, I really don't know why I'm laughing. Nerves, I guess. The most unusual thing to me was Stella and Sean, and then finding out that she was your sister! What an unlikely pair!"

She grimaced. "How do you think I feel?! I tried my best to talk her out of it, but even though she looks timid, she's got quite a wild streak. Ugh, and that puppy dog look in her eyes when she looks at him! I want to rip her eyeballs right out and knock some sense into her!"

We both chuckled, equally appalled that anyone, least of all her sister, would be interested in Sean.

"I've got to be on my way. Are you going to be okay?"

I nodded in return. "Yes, Nathan should be back

soon. He's gone to speak with his family, so I don't imagine he'll be in good spirits."

Not knowing how to respond, Lynette quietly left after thanking me for the coffee and the information. Alone, with my emotions running amuck, I finally had a good cry then curled up with both cats for a nap.

Hummer's tail was still fat.

———————

It was almost dark when Nathan woke me with a gentle kiss on my cheek, then sank down onto the couch next to me. We sat quietly awhile before I mustered the courage to tell him of my discovery earlier that day. Tears slid down my cheeks as I told him, and the horror on his face burned a hole into my mind that I knew would never heal. I watched his Adam's apple bob several times before he spoke. "It's not your fault, Amalia. I'm sure there's a long list of people out there who had a grudge against my sister. Trust me, I know I, and the rest of my family too, will be at the top of the suspect list. I think that we need to get over to Georgina's place to try to get some answers. Are you feeling up to it?"

I wasn't, but I knew that the quicker we had information, the quicker this case would be solved, and the quicker we'd begin to heal. I squared my shoulders, swiped angrily at my nose, and then nodded my head. "Absolutely! But first, tell me how it went with your family?"

He shrugged. "Everyone seemed to be in shock.

Officer Sean had sent someone to let Mom and Dad know, and they were in the process of calling all of us kids when I arrived. Everyone rushed over, and then I shared what I knew. Mom nearly collapsed." He paused to regain his composure while I rubbed his back, trying to comfort him.

"Do they hate me?" I asked softly.

"They did wonder what type of place this was and why you were involved. Of course I explained that you weren't. Let's just go, Amalia; I'm anxious to see what Georgina can tell us."

It's time for a food break!

I make these three recipes at the same time since a lot of the ingredients are the same. This way, I only have to chop the same things once and the meals for the next three to four days are complete. They reheat well and the two meat dishes freeze well.

Chicken/Turkey meat-stuffed lettuce or pita wraps (note: use meat mixture three ways! See below for some great options)

- 1 small package ground chicken or turkey (or both and use ½ of each in each dish)
- 1 tablespoon olive oil
- ½ small red bell pepper, diced
- 5 garlic cloves diced medium
- ½ small onion diced medium
- ½ small carrot and ½ celery stalk, diced small
- Few sprigs of chopped fresh cilantro, chives and parsley or ½ teaspoon dried of each
- ½ teaspoon of garlic powder and chili powder
- 2 dashes of turmeric and cayenne

Combine following in a glass before adding to rest:

- 1 tablespoon low sodium soya sauce
- 1 tablespoon Pad Thai sauce or any other favourite, similar type sauce

- 1 teaspoon cornstarch
- ¾ cup cold water

Serve on: full lettuce leaves or pita

Place meat and olive oil in a skillet and cook until no longer pink. Add all of the vegetables and cook another couple of minutes then add all the herbs and spices. Cook another minute, then add all other ingredients except for the lettuce/pita. Simmer on low heat for about 10-15 minutes. If mixture gets a bit too thick, just add a dash more water.

I use this recipe three ways, so I divide the final product into three portions, and freeze the other two portions to use later.

First way to enjoy: Place hot mixture onto lettuce leaves and roll like a "wrap" or make pita sandwiches.

Second way to enjoy: Place hot mixture over top the Orzo dish that follows. Also excellent on rice.

Third way to enjoy: Hand pies!

Additional ingredients for hand pies:

- Pie crust
- 1/2 cup shredded cheese of your choice
- Meat mixture from above
- 1 egg

For this, you'll need a pie crust of your choice, whether it's homemade or store bought. Allow crust/

dough to thaw at room temperature (usually about half an hour to an hour), roll it out a bit to make it slightly bigger, then cut down the middle and then across in the middle (i.e.: into four equal sections).

Place a good heaping tablespoon of meat mixture into the middle of each triangle of dough. If using cheese, place some on top of the meat mixture. Next, fold over so that all the edges of the dough meet up and seal the edges by pressing down all around with a fork.

Place the four hand pies on a baking sheet lined with parchment paper and brush the top of each with an egg (just mix up egg in a bowl and brush a thin coating onto pies). Poke each top a few times with a fork to allow the steam to escape.

Bake at 400 degrees on the middle rack for about 15 minutes, until the pies are a lovely golden-brown colour. If your oven usually burns things or runs hot, you may wish to bake at 375 degrees.

Chicken/Turkey Meatball Submarines

- 1 small package ground chicken or turkey (or both and use ½ of each in each dish)

- 1 egg

- ¼ cup breadcrumbs (or use 1 piece of fresh or slightly stale sliced bread torn up into little pieces—if doing this method then mix the bread and egg together and let soak a few minutes before adding to the rest of recipe)

- 5 garlic cloves diced small

- ½ small onion diced small

- Few sprigs of chopped fresh cilantro and parsley or ½ teaspoon dried

- 1 teaspoon Italian seasoning or oregano

- ½ teaspoon salt

- A few shakes of pepper to taste

- 1 jar of your favourite, good quality marinara/spaghetti sauce or make your own

- 4 of your favourite buns (ciabatta, mini-baguette, panini, etc)

- 4 tablespoons of your favourite cheese, grated

Pre-heat oven to 425. Line a baking dish with parchment paper (it just makes life easier).

Mix all the ingredients except for the sauce and buns then make meatballs out of about 1 tablespoon of meat. Bake for 13 minutes, flip them over then bake another 12 minutes.

Meanwhile, heat up your sauce of choice. Once the meatballs are done, place into the sauce and let simmer for ten minutes

Slice the buns down the middle and place around five to six meatballs into each. Use as much or little sauce as you want. If using cheese, top each with about one tablespoon of cheese, then broil in oven for a couple of minutes, watching closely so that it doesn't burn.

Leftover meatballs/sauce can be served over the following Orzo dish or used to make more submarine sandwiches.

Citrus & Garlic Orzo

- 1 ½ cup orzo pasta

- 1 tablespoon olive oil

- 3 cups of low or no sodium chicken broth (if using no-sodium broth, you will have to add salt to your liking). You can also just use water instead of broth and about ½ to 1 teaspoons of salt

- 1 tablespoon of lime or lemon juice

- 5 gloves of garlic diced small and ½ teaspoon garlic powder

- ¼ teaspoon dried basil or a few sprigs fresh, chopped (I use Lime Basil, a somewhat rare variety that I grow in my herb garden)

- Several shakes of black pepper

- A few sprigs of fresh cilantro, parsley and chives, chopped or ½ teaspoon of each, dried

On medium heat, combine orzo and olive oil. Stir constantly to lightly toast. When at least 1/3rd of the orzo is toasted add all of the remaining ingredients. Stir, reduce heat to simmer (low), cover and cook until the liquid is almost all absorbed (stir every few minutes). When almost all liquid is absorbed (about 15-20 minutes), turn off stove and allow orzo to sit, covered, for another ten minutes.

Delicious on its own or with suggestions above.

Chapter Six

Having known her for many years, it was easy for Nathan to track down Georgina and we were soon in the posh Kanata Lakes area, ringing her doorbell. She peeked out the side window and, recognizing Nathan, opened the door for us, immediately bursting into tears and throwing herself at him for a hug.

"Hello Georgie," he managed to muffle into her massive hair that covered his face, barely avoiding ingesting it. I suppressed a giggle, as the timing was highly inappropriate.

"Oh, Nathan, how utterly devastating! I'm so sorry for your loss. And for my loss... She was my best friend, of course, and I just can't believe this has happened. One minute we're sitting there, eating and laughing, and the next, she's just...gone." The words tumbled from her mouth until a sob caught in her throat, and I could see Nathan swallowing furiously around the lump in his own throat.

"Thank you, Georgie. I'm still in shock. Do you mind if we ask you a few questions?" She looked at me, question marks flashing in her own tear-filled eyes.

"I'm sorry, this is Amalia," said Nathan. "She's the owner at the bistro, and she's also my girlfriend. I was there last night, but I didn't see you. I did see Merri though, after…" This time, the tears got the better of him.

"Come, let's sit down." She led us into her living room. "The police were here this afternoon, with more questions. I imagine you might have similar ones."

"When did she come back to Robin, Georgie? And more importantly, do you know why?"

She let out a big sigh. "I don't know for certain, but she'd loosely kept in touch over the past few years. I know she was deeply ashamed for the way she left town, and what she'd done before leaving. Before you ask, she did not 'borrow' money from me. When I found out she was in town, I called her. She was hoping to make amends with the family but unsure how to approach everyone, or who to approach first. I thought a nice evening out would take her mind off things, so I treated her to the wine and cheese tasting last night. I thought it would be a great opportunity for us to catch up, but she spent the entire time fixated on her phone."

I racked my brain. Had I noticed anyone preoccupied with their phone? It's something I might have noticed, since it is a pet-peeve of mine, but this particular incident did not stand out in my mind.

"Why did you choose the bistro for your outing?" His tone was casual, but I knew how important the answer was to him. He wanted to make sure she hadn't known we were dating, and hadn't singled me out for some reason.

"My brother lives in the area and had mentioned it, having been there a number of times. He highly recommended it."

"Your brother?" Nathan exclaimed sharply, making us both jump. "I thought you and Giorgio barely spoke?"

I could not hide a grimace. Their parents had named them Giorgio and Georgina?

"We don't, really. It's a sporadic relationship. We sometimes text one another. I haven't actually seen him in a few years, and I don't even know exactly where he lives, although he had mentioned he lived close to the Ottawa River in the town of Robin."

I could relate to what she was saying. That was the type of relationship my own brother and I had, with the exception that we did see each other at least a couple of times a year. I knew firsthand that just because someone was family it was not a guarantee that you were close.

"Did Merri appear to be afraid in any way?"

She frowned, deep in thought. "She was jumpy, but not necessarily afraid."

"Did she happen to mention with whom she was texting?" Nathan asked.

"Not exactly. But she did say that she was dealing with some important issues, and mentioned that Alan had contacted her, asking her to meet with him and his lawyer regarding divorce proceedings, but I don't think that she was texting with him last night. She likely would have mentioned that since she'd mentioned the divorce."

"Divorce? You mean they hadn't divorced years ago when she left?"

"My understanding is that she left him without warning, just like everyone else she left behind. He must have heard she was back in town and wanted closure to their relationship. I believe she had actually agreed to meet him sometime later this week. I suppose we should let him know…" Her voice trailed. She didn't want to appear as though she was volunteering for the task.

"Don't worry, Georgie. I'll make sure the police advise him."

"Thank you, Nathan. Actually, I don't think I mentioned that to the police during our conversation."

A few moments of silence followed before I worked up the courage to speak. "When she went to the bathroom, did she make any comments beforehand or seem more agitated?"

"No, there was nothing out of the ordinary about that. She just said she had to pee and would be right back. She did mention she was having a great time, and thanked me for bringing her." This brought a tremulous little smile to Georgina's lips.

"She took her phone with her, but not her purse. What woman goes to the bathroom without her purse?"

Nathan and I exchanged a look. I tested my memory, trying to recall if I had noticed a cell phone in the bathroom when I'd peered inside. I was pretty sure that Nathan was doing the same, but we both remained silent.

Out of questions, Nathan exchanged phone numbers with her, promising to keep in touch and to let her know the details of the funeral arrangements. Back inside the car, he was the first to speak: "Did you notice a cell phone in the bathroom?"

"No, but I only had a quick look. Though I'm quite sure that I didn't notice anyone texting excessively during the wine tasting. We'll have to be sure to mention all this to Officer Lynette, in case Georgina didn't, as well as the information about her husband."

"Yes, let's do that tomorrow. It's already late and I'm exhausted." His features were quite drawn from sadness, stress and the burden of looking into Merri's death.

Back at home, we took the exterior stairs to my living quarters, avoiding having to go into the bistro. No sooner were we settled with a glass of wine when a knock at the door commanded our attention. I peered out the window, surprised to see Stephen there at this late hour. "Come in, what's up?"

"I was worried about you, Sis," he purred with faux concern. I knew him better than that. He certainly would not be worried; amused or even delighted by the misfortune that had come my way, perhaps, but certainly not worried. "I heard about what happened last night, plus the break-in. I came by earlier, but you weren't here."

"How did you hear about last night?" I asked, already suspecting what the answer would be.

"I picked up a pizza at Leonardo's earlier today and overheard some talk."

Considering my feud with Leonardo, it would be just like him to rub salt into a wound. He'd add vinegar, too. And Sriracha sauce!

"Mom and Dad are beside themselves with worry," he continued. Of course, he would have been the one to mention it to them.

I cut him off at this point. "Yes, well, please have some respect. The victim was Nathan's sister. And Nathan happens to be my boyfriend." Stephen had nodded to him when he entered the room, but neither had bothered to introduce themselves and this was the first opportunity I'd had.

He was slightly embarrassed. "I'm so sorry. I won't bother you right now. Can I just use your bathroom before I go?" With that he shuffled down the hallway. Why he couldn't hold his bladder for the two minutes it would take to get back to my parents' place was beyond me.

"I don't like him," Nathan stated flatly.

"Yeah, well, I often don't either," I replied quietly. There were times over the years that we actually got along, like when he helped me move into the bistro, but those moments were always short-lived and few and far between. The older we got, the more infrequent the good times seemed to be.

"Alright, Sis, I'll be going now. Maybe I'll stop by tomorrow to see how you're doing. I'll be in town for a few days. I was going to ask if I could sleep in your spare room, but considering all the recent events, I think I'll just hang out with Mom and Dad." He gave me a kiss on the cheek, nodded to Nathan, and then took his leave.

"I'm going to take a shower then get ready for bed," I said to Nathan.

"I'll do the same once you're done. I'll tidy up out here so you don't have to. I have to keep busy," he mumbled more to himself than to me.

I shuffled to the bathroom, PJs tucked underneath my arm, then stopped in my tracks. The shower curtain was partially open. I knew I had not left it like that. Being slightly OCD, having a partially open or completely open shower curtain would irritate me. What had Stephen been doing in here?

I also noticed that one side of the vanity cabinet was slightly ajar. Opening the cabinet underneath the sink, it seemed that things were slightly out of place. Perhaps it was Nathan; after all, he'd been here since the day before and he wasn't especially tidy. His offer to straighten up had surprised me.

I shrugged it aside for now and took a long, steamy shower. By the time I got out, I had forgotten about things having been amiss, especially when Nathan stepped into the bathroom buck naked and ready for his shower. The grin froze on my lips as I remembered the death of his sister. I gave him a chaste peck on the cheek and then allowed him his privacy. By the time he joined me in bed, I was sound asleep, with a cat on either side of me.

Chapter Seven

"So, are you going to tell me about this little guy here?" Nathan asked around a mouth full of fur. The kitten was sound asleep on his chest, while Hummer lounged above my head, his tail curled downward onto my neck. It was no longer fat, but perhaps that's because he was sound asleep. His snores rumbled gently at the top of my head.

"That's true, you haven't seen him yet! He was off exploring when you got up yesterday morning and I hadn't thought to mention him. He wandered in a couple of days ago, the day of the break-in, since the door was open. Honestly, I can barely remember; so much has happened since then. Anyway, he was pretty hungry and there's no other houses close by. He's such a sweetheart, and I think Hummer is actually getting used to him. Of course, if I hear of anyone missing a kitten, I'll step forward."

I could, of course, have posted a notice inside the bistro, or at the corner store, regarding a found kitten, but I pushed my pesky conscience aside. The little guy was clearly happy here, and he was very young. If he'd had a home and was able to wander off, with the highway so close, then the owners clearly weren't watching him carefully enough, so he'd be much safer with me. My conscience was happy with that theory.

We watched in horror as the kitten jumped off Nathan's chest and made its way toward Hummer. He licked his head a couple of times, then curled up tightly against him, immediately falling asleep. Hummer merely glared at him with one open eye then returned to his own slumber.

"I can't believe it," I whispered to Nate.

"What are you going to call him? Or is it her?"

"Good question. First, I have to find out what sex it is. It's so young, I can't quite tell; although I think it's a boy. I have to book an appointment with the vet for vaccinations…" My voice trailed as I mentally added up the money it would cost; money I didn't really have to spare.

We slipped out of bed cautiously, so as not to wake the cats. We'd no sooner settled onto the couch with our morning coffees when an incessant knocking sounded at the door.

I looked at Nathan in horror. My father had that special, woodpecker way of knocking. "Unless you want to meet my dad, I suggest you go back to bed for a while."

He looked at me in alarm before dashing down the hall to the bedroom. Under normal circumstances, it would have been quite comical, but this wasn't the time for introductions, even though, no doubt, he'd heard from Stephen that Nathan had stayed overnight at my place.

I opened the door and he stormed inside. My hackles rose in self-defence, certain I knew what was coming.

"Bazd meg, Amalia!" He began his rant, using the Hungarian equivalent to the English F-word. Instinctively, I raised my hands in protest. "She's done it again." He walked over to my coffee maker and poured himself a cup of coffee before joining me on the couch. I was motionless, my hands still raised but no longer sure what his rant was about.

"She? Who? What has *she* done? Not me?"

"Your mother has signed us up for pole dancing. Again!"

I burst out laughing, louder than I should have, but my nerves were still on edge and I was so relieved to hear that his anger wasn't directed at me.

A while back, my mother had thought she was signing them up for Polish dancing, but instead it was for a pole dancing class. I had been the lucky one to join her, and now she'd made the same mistake. Or was it intentional?!

"Relax, Dad. Just go to the community centre and explain the mistake. I'm sure they'll understand and refund the money, or let you sign up for something else." I patted his arm, noticing how scrawny it had become as he'd aged.

"I'm not going pole dancing," he insisted vehemently, causing me to burst out laughing again.

"Well, don't look at me; I'm not going either!"

"Maybe your nice friend Nora would like to go with Mama," my dad said hopefully. I knew he was envisioning her in that silly push-up bra she used to wear when she'd left her husband and was messing around with Mr. Leonardo. I still shuddered at the memory.

"Dad, listen: no one is going pole dancing." He nodded sullenly then perked up.

"Stephen said something happened here the other day?" The spark in his eyes returned, causing me to frown. About four months had now passed since he had *help*ed me investigate the last incident that had occurred at the bistro. Clearly, he'd enjoyed himself, if his sparkling eyes were any indication.

"You're not getting involved this time, Dad. That's probably why Mom was trying to sign you up for dancing class—as your punishment for getting involved last time. And I certainly don't want Mom to be mad at me for involving you and then quit."

Once a week, due to popular demand, my mum helped out at the bistro. It got her out of the house, and although she found it tiring, the compliments she got for her specialty were very rewarding for her. Truth be told, I was overjoyed to get a weekly schnitzel fix. Although I knew how to make it, I seldom fried food, but had no qualms eating it if someone else did the greasy work.

"Are *you* getting involved?" he asked me point-blank.

I nodded sullenly. "Yes, Dad; I have to. The victim was my boyfriend's sister."

"Where is he?" Dad asked, craning his neck as though Nathan would magically appear from behind the couch. "Stephen said he was here late last night."

"He's still sleeping. He's quite distraught. He saw his sister's body. This probably isn't a good time to meet him." I almost feared he'd march down the hallway to my bedroom to introduce himself. He stood, and my jaw dropped in horror.

"Okay, I will go now. Call me if you need me." He'd taken his leave in English, which unnerved me. Usually, I spoke Hungarian with my parents, so anytime they said anything in English, it momentarily confused me. I replied partially in Hungarian, partially in English, and a spattering of French too, attempting to say goodbye and that I'd be in touch. It came out completely garbled, but he was used to it.

Once the door closed, I bellowed. "Coast is clear, Nathan!" I waited a few moments, expecting him to shuffle down the hallway. When I got no response, I went to get him, but instead found him curled up with Hummer and the kitten, fast asleep.

Smiling, I tucked the blanket gently around him then quietly got ready to run errands. Assuming I'd be able to re-open the bistro the next day, I had cheese and salamis to purchase. I scribbled a quick note for Nathan, letting him know where I had gone, as well as a reminder that he had to call Officer Lynette, and then went on my way.

Chapter Eight

I was loaded down with bags of food as I reached my car and fumbled for my keys at the bottom of my purse. A ball of mozzarella somehow escaped one of the bags and proceeded to roll across the parking lot. To my surprise, a brown-haired woman took off in hot pursuit, stopping the cheese just before it rolled under a car. I still stood there, with one hand in my purse and the other holding all the bags as Stella trudged over to me, cheese held firmly in both hands as though it were a delicate, crystal ball.

"Well, that was my exercise for the day!" She giggled, plopping the cheese back inside a bag.

"Thank you, Stella," I grinned, her giggle contagious. "It's nice to see you again."

To my surprise, she asked if I'd like to join her for coffee, indicating that she was just about to head into the coffee shop located next to the deli that I'd just exited. I accepted, strangely drawn to her and also too curious about her to refuse.

"I'd love to join you, though I can't stay long."

A few minutes later, we snagged the only seats available. We sipped happily on our pumpkin spice lattes and munched in comfortable silence on pumpkin scones. For some reason, I was completely at ease with her. Nevertheless, I was here for a reason. I snickered softly, audible only to my own ears; let the questioning begin.

I was just opening my mouth to speak when she beat me to it.

"How are you holding up through all this?"

"I'm okay. Stressed, of course, but mostly worried about my boyfriend," I replied.

"Your boyfriend? Has something happened to him?" She looked confused.

"Well, yes. The man with me that evening, the one who was very upset, is the brother of the victim." Clearly, Officer Sean hadn't told her a thing.

"Are you saying she was murdered?" This was exclaimed rather loudly, causing some heads to turn our way. "Sean just said that there was an incident in the customer washroom and that the lady was taken to the hospital." Her eyes seemed to sparkle just as my dad's had. What the heck?

"So, what happened to her? Did you see the body? How's your boyfriend coping with this? Oh, this is so exciting! I can't believe I was somewhere where someone was murdered. This is almost the craziest thing that's ever happened to me!"

'Almost,' I thought to myself?

What a delightfully odd little creature she was!

The demure look did not match her enthusiastic, inquisitive and bubbly personality. I found myself liking her more and more with each passing minute. But, clearly, I wouldn't be able to pump her for any information, since she was completely clueless. That thought actually helped me to relax, knowing I could simply be myself, enjoy her company and not have to be in 'detective mode.'

"Unfortunately, I did see her. And her brother took it quite hard; he'd seen her too, recognized her immediately since she was wearing a top that he'd given her."

The full implication of my words was not lost on her and she gasped, eyes wide with fascination. "Do you mean that, other than the top, it would have been hard to identify her?"

"I probably shouldn't be mentioning any of this. Sean doesn't really care for me, and I don't want to upset him by sharing information that I shouldn't." She looked at me with her doe eyes and I burst out laughing. "I'm kidding. I don't really care if he gets mad at me. I don't like him very much. Maybe I should mention that he dated my best friend for a short time, and it didn't end well."

To my surprise, she nodded. "Oh yes, that I do know. When I told him that I wanted our first date to be at your bistro, he tried to talk me out of it and finally admitted that he'd dated your friend. I can be stubborn though, and I didn't let him squirm out of it. Actually, it just made me all the more determined."

She smiled a brilliant smile, obviously proud of herself.

We continued to chat for the next hour, staying far longer than I'd originally planned. I was captivated by this woman. She was witty, strong willed, and obviously intelligent. She shared that she was a computer programmer and ran the IT division at a company in Ottawa.I was impressed.

As we exchanged anecdotes from our childhoods, she suddenly frowned.

"I have to get back to work. I've stayed long past my lunch break. But ever since you mentioned that the lady was murdered, something has been niggling at my mind, but I couldn't put my finger on it. But it has just come to me. I remember now that I saw someone leaving–I didn't think anything of it at the time–but I remember looking in the direction of the door, since I was waiting for Sean. And just minutes before he arrived, I think I saw someone just as the door was closing. I can't even tell you if it was male or female, but I remember a dark coat." She frowned again as she tried to delve deeper into her memory. Her eyes sparkled, knowing she had very likely seen the killer.

"Stella, you have to tell Sean! Maybe they crossed paths in the parking lot since Sean arrived shortly after that. Maybe it'll spark Sean's memory."

We finished the last sips of coffee and exchanged phone numbers, promising to keep in touch. I smiled at my new friend as we parted ways and chuckled to myself. Sean wasn't going to like this one bit; and naturally, that made me enjoy it all the more.

I returned to find Nathan and the cats sipping coffee in the living room. Likely, Hummer was waiting to lick the cup as he liked coffee. I didn't know about the kitten yet. I gave Nathan a long hug then placed a scone on the coffee table in front of him. His face lit up ever so slightly at the sight of the little treat, then darkened again when I shared Stella's news with him.

"It's not much of a clue," he groused. "Pretty much everyone owns a dark coat. Hopefully, Officer Sean saw something on his way inside." He ran his fingers through his curly hair in frustration. "I have to go back to Kingston, since I hadn't expected to be here more than a couple of days. Will you be okay?"

"Of course; I'll be fine. I've been through this before, Nathan. You have nothing to worry about. You wouldn't happen to have Alan's address, would you? Did you call Officer Lynette to tell her about him?"

"No, I haven't called yet." He gave me a long look. "As far as I know, he still lives in the house where he and my sister lived. Perhaps I'll wait until tomorrow before calling Lynette, to give you a chance to pay him a visit. Although, maybe it would be best if I were to go with you," his voice faltered, unsure what to do.

"Nathan, maybe it's best that you don't. If you and Alan haven't kept in touch since Merri left, he might not feel comfortable sharing information with you about your sister. I'll simply tell him I'm investigating the case for you. People usually assume that I'm a private investigator and seldom ask for credentials. Trust me; I want to help you."

He nodded. "Just promise me you'll be careful, okay? Alan's a pretty quiet guy, very bookish and quite meek, which is the only reason I'm agreeing to this. Still, I'd feel better if you had someone with you."

My mind already racing ahead, I wondered who would be my trusty backup for this adventure.

The answer surprised even me.

Chapter Nine

It was almost supper time when Nathan left, promising to text me once he arrived safely in Kingston. No sooner did his jeep leave my parking lot than I was on the phone with Nicole.

"What are you doing tomorrow around lunchtime?" Forgetting my manners, I came right to the point. We'd known each other since the age of twelve, so she was accustomed to it.

"Well, hello, Amalia. How are you? What's new with you? I'm doing well, thank you," she replied in a playful yet sarcastic tone. I then realized that she didn't know about the most recent events at the bistro. I quickly filled her in.

"Damn, I'd love to insvestigate with you, but I have a lunch date with Drew and then I have to go to work."

Drew was a friend of Nathan's and she'd met him the same night that I'd met Nathan. I smiled, happy for her. It was her longest relationship in years and clearly she was over the fiasco with Officer Sean.

Next, I tried Nora, this time remembering my manners, asking how she was, then telling her the latest news.

"Oh, Amalia! I would love to help you tomorrow, but Craig and I have a couples counselling session. I don't think I need it, but he certainly does." The disappointment in her voice was evident. Nora had helped me a number of times in the past and had even lived with me for a short while when she had left Craig due to a mid-life crisis. I grinned at the memory, since Nora was clearly past the middle of any normal life, and well into her fifties or early sixties. Nora was my Betty White; short, grey-haired, and sharp as a tack. "I'll be there for opening time at the bistro though. I'd rebook the appointment but Craig is very serious about our counselling sessions. The other day, he even hinted that perhaps I'm getting too old to help you out at the bistro. Can you imagine? I'm nowhere near old. You'd think he'd be happy that I recently retired from my day job but still keep myself busy. I think he just doesn't like that Leo is so close to the bistro; he's afraid I'll be tempted, but he won't admit it. He's having a hard time getting over that."

I shuddered at the memory of Nora's tryst with the nasty Mr. Leonardo. I will never, to my dying day, understand what she saw in him during her brief separation from her husband.

After hanging up, I considered my remaining options. I didn't want to involve Chloé; I was very protective of her. Barely over 21 and ten years my junior, I felt an odd maternal instinct toward her. Although Alan was reportedly a very mild and meek man, I had to remember that, as Merri's husband, he would be a prime suspect. I didn't want to endanger her again. It had happened before and I had felt incredibly guilty. Plus, on top of working full time, she'd recently started taking night classes at a local college, so I knew she'd have her plate full.

Stella? I thought she'd likely get a kick out of it, but I didn't know her well enough yet.

That left only one person; my dad, despite the speech I'd given him earlier. I gave him a call and almost swore when my mother answered the phone. We made small talk before I casually asked to speak to my father. When she asked me why, I racked my brains for a plausible excuse. "Well, my sink has a leak and I can't seem to fix it."

"Oh, we'll come over right away," she started to reply before I quickly spoke up.

"No, Mum, no. It's okay, it can wait until tomorrow." Darn, I'd chosen a horrible excuse and now she wanted to come over. "To be honest, I have a migraine, so I was just about to lie down." The last thing I needed was for her to come over as well, and see that there was no leak. Finally, she put him on the phone.

"Dad, I hate to ask, but could you come with me tomorrow to interrogate a suspect?" I could envision his eyes shining.

"Tomorrow? Oh, sonovagun! I could be there later

in the afternoon. We have to go to yoga class." The pain in his voice was evident.

"Yoga?" I exclaimed. "Since when do you do yoga? And why?"

"It's in place of the pole-dancing class. It's the only class they still had room in and Mama won't let me stay home." I had to resist the urge to laugh as I pictured him in a yoga class. I was familiar with the classes in question since it was the same ones that I'd taken in recent months.

What in the world would he wear? I envisioned his favourite brown pants and yellow shirt, stifling a giggle, then politely declined his offer to help me later in the day as it would be too close to opening time at the bistro. "By the way, I told mom that my sink had a leak, just as a cover story."

"Okay, you call plumber, bye-bye," my dad's voice rose so that my mom could hear.

We hung up, and against my better judgement I brushed my conscience aside and called Chloé, who was thrilled by the prospect to help but had to decline as she had to work during the day then also at night for me. Out of options, it looked like I would be on my own the next day.

As I sat contemplating my next move, Chloé's words sunk in. She'd be at work. Nicole would be at work. That meant, more than likely Alan would be at work too. I tended to forget that other people did not work the same hours or days that I did. I glanced at the clock. It was 7:15 p.m. now. Before I could change my mind, I grabbed my purse and a coat and headed to my car.

20 minutes later, I pulled up in front of Alan's house. As I was walking to the door, a man emerged from the house and I braced myself. Was this Alan? As the man walked toward his car and I continued toward the house, we came almost face to face before we both stopped in our tracks.

"You!" We both exclaimed at the same time. "What are you doing here?" Again, we both spoke the same words at the same time.

Before I knew what was happening, Mr. Leonardo opened his car door and reached inside. Out of sheer instinct, I moved a few feet away, but I was too slow. Moments later, a bat of pepperoni came sailing through the air and knocked me on the side of the cheek with a sharp sting, his strong, pizza-dough-pounding hands having thrown it with quite a force.

As it bounced to the ground, I stooped to pick it up. I resisted the urge to pummel him with it; it would serve a better purpose in my belly. I tucked it safely into my pocket, part of it sticking out due to the length.

"Why do you keep doing that?" I squawked.

"There's always trouble with you around," he barked at me. Out of the corner of my eye, I could see another person getting out of the car, but I dared not take my eyes off Leonardo. What kind of lunatic drives around with bats of pepperoni?

"Missy? Is that you?" There were only two people that called me Missy, and this one was female.

"Mrs. Knuedle? What in the world?"

"Leo, leave this poor girl alone. What's wrong with you, throwing your meat at her?"

He almost looked embarrassed, but in the end, he continued to glare at me.

"I didn't realize the two of you knew each other." I aimed this remark at Mrs. Knuedle.

"We've been dating for a couple of months now," she replied, looking smug, like a cat that just caught a chipmunk. "What are you doing here, Missy?"

"I came to speak to Alan about something. My boyfriend, Nathan, is related to him."

"Nathan?" Mr. Leonardo now joined the conversation. "Large, double meat, extra cheese?"

"How in the world would you know that?"

"I only have one customer named Nathan, and that's what he always orders. Ha! No more pizza for you." At that, he spit on the ground and narrowly missed my shoe.

Mrs. Knuedle looked at me shrewdly. "I heard about what happened at the bistro. Is that why you're here?"

Mrs. Knuedle usually worked as an undercover agent, and we'd collaborated on a case a few months back. An idea began to form.

"Yes, but it would appear that I don't have backup. You wouldn't by chance be interested in joining me?"

"Oh, that might be interesting. I've been on an extended vacation for a few weeks and I'm getting a bit antsy. Fill me in while we walk to the door."

Overjoyed by my luck, I quickly told her as much

as I could as we moved toward the door. I could hear Leo muttering to himself behind us, clearly not happy with the situation.

With a shaky hand, I rang the doorbell and waited nervously. This wasn't something I enjoyed doing. Heck, it wasn't even something that I was always good at, but when the bistro's reputation was at stake, I had no choice. Since the victim had been Nathans' sister, I was all the more motivated.

The door flung open. "It's about time…." He broke off, clearly expecting someone other than us. "Oh, sorry… May I help you?"

"We don't mean to disturb you at this late hour, but we're here about your ex-wife, Merri. We'd like to ask you some questions."

His features became rigid; he did not look meek or timid. "Are you police officers?" Damn, I was hoping he wouldn't ask that, but Mrs. Knuedle was quick to respond.

"Yes. This will just take a few minutes." With that, she took her badge out of her coat pocket for him to see. I merely stood there, smiling politely. To my relief, he nodded and let us inside rather than ask to see my non-existent credentials. He did glance curiously at the pepperoni sticking out of my pocket but refrained from commenting.

He led us into the living room, smiling sheepishly at the pizza, plates and lit candles set out on the floor in front of the fireplace. "I'm expecting company, ladies, so can we keep this brief?"

The aroma of the pizza reached my nostrils and I began to drool. At the same time, my phone began to ring. Apologizing, I quickly muted it, and then glanced at Mrs. Knuedle, who nodded at me to begin. Suddenly, I realized that Alan might not yet know of Merri's death and I faltered, suddenly unsure where to begin.

"Have you heard about Merri's unfortunate...circumstances?" I bumbled.

"You people really don't communicate with each other, do you?" He chuckled. "I take it you're not the officers that called me earlier today? I thought you would be visiting me tomorrow."

"My apologies and my condolences, Sir," I replied gently so as not to further upset him.

He waved my comments aside. "No condolences required. We've been separated for years. She was supposed to meet with me to sign the divorce papers, but I suppose that won't be necessary now. It's a shame I had already spent the money on a lawyer. Oh, I realize my comment may seem cold, but you have to understand, she left without explanation years ago. She left a note saying that the marriage was over and that she was moving far away."

"Didn't you ever try to contact her?"

"Sure. Countless times. But she never answered my calls, or emails, or texts. I eventually gave up. No one knew where she'd gone, otherwise I would have served her divorce papers long ago."

"When, and how, did you become aware that she was back in town?"

"A mutual friend had seen her downtown and had immediately contacted me to let me know. To my amazement, she had never changed her cellphone number, and this time she responded to the text I sent her. She agreed to meet with my lawyer and me to sign the divorce papers."

"When was this supposed to have taken place?"

"This coming Friday."

"Have you seen her since her return?" Mrs. Knuedle jumped in with the question.

"No, she refused to meet. In fact, she didn't even want me to be present at the meeting with my lawyer, but I stood firm on that. I had to get closure, see her one last time, have her face me and possibly tell me why she left. I thought our marriage was just fine; we never even fought. Well, not really. For all I know, maybe she didn't even plan to show up."

"Can you tell us where you were on the evening of the murder?"

"I was here at home, and before you ask, no, I have no witnesses. My car is always parked in my garage, so unless the neighbours noticed me getting home from work and parking in the garage, I'm afraid I have no witnesses. I did not go anywhere that evening and, in fact, I even went to bed early as I've not slept well of late and I was exhausted. If you don't mind, will there be any more questions? As mentioned, I am expecting company and it would be awfully embarrassing to have police officers here…"

"That's all for today, Sir. Thank you for your time.

Do expect to answer more questions, as they arise, please." Mrs. Knuedle warned him gently, knowing full well that some officers would likely show up the next day. He nodded as he walked us to the door.

"Ladies, before you leave, a quick question, if I may? Officer," he addressed me, "I must know, why is there a pepperoni in your pocket?"

I said the first thing that came to mind. "I'm in training. I'm not allowed to carry a gun yet." With that, we took our leave, Mrs. Knuedle's giggles finally getting the better of her once Alan had firmly closed the door.

"Oh Missy, you make me laugh. I'd better call this in to the office to let them know before they show up tomorrow. Maybe they'll be satisfied with the information that I'll relay."

"I hope you don't get into trouble on my account," I said.

She waved my apology aside. "Nothing I can't handle. Take care, Missy. I hope you learned something helpful from Alan."

She climbed into Leo's car as he glared at me from the driver's seat. I smiled sweetly and gave the pepperoni in my pocket a loving stroke as he peeled out of the driveway.

I, on the other hand, climbed into my car and drove only a few houses away, hoping to catch a glimpse of Alan's expected date.

I was not disappointed.

Chapter Ten

Just minutes after we had left, a car sped onto Alan's driveway, screeching to a halt only inches from the house. Despite the darkness, there was no mistaking the giant head of bushy hair of his date–Georgie. My stomach turned. Georgie was dating her supposed best friend's husband? This certainly cast a new light on everything.

Proud of myself, I hurried home, wondering how to tell Nathan about this new development. I sensed that this information would be pivotal to the case, but knew Nathan would be shocked by it.

Safely home, I was greeted by both cats milling anxiously around my feet. The food bowl was empty and they were hungry, although they appeared to be getting along amicably. Hummer hadn't eaten the kitten, so that was a good sign. All the same, I filled two separate bowls and put one in front of each, then settled down to jot down my findings and contact Nathan.

To my surprise, I realized I had a voice message from Nathan and remembered the call I'd gotten when I had been at Alan's. Listening to the message, my face grew rigid with concern. Someone had tried to run Nathan off the 401 highway that led to Kingston. With shaky hands, I quickly called him back.

"Nathan, I'm so happy to hear your voice."

"I'm okay. Remember, I drive a Jeep. Maybe I'm being paranoid, but I'm sure it wasn't an accident. Someone cut in front of me quickly, but I managed to swerve to avoid them. I ended up on the median before gaining control of the vehicle; and by then the car had exited the highway and I lost sight of it. I didn't even get a plate number or the make of car, it all happened so fast."

"I'm glad you are okay. No whiplash or anything?"

"Nothing. I slowed down but didn't slam on the brakes. All is well. I reported the incident to the police, and mentioned that my sister was recently murdered, in case there's a connection. I'm back in Kingston now. Is everything okay over there?"

"I went to see Alan today."

"I thought you were going to do that tomorrow. Who was your backup?"

"Well, believe it or not—and it's a long story—but it was Mrs. Knuedle! Remember her from a few months back, when Milton's wife was poisoned? I have to say, we make a pretty good pair. Anyway, since she's an actual police officer, it made the questioning easy. First thing he did was ask if we were officers. I honestly don't think he would have answered any questions otherwise." I quickly filled him in on the details. "After the interrogation ended, I parked a few houses away, hoping to catch a glimpse of his date. Nathan; it was Georgie!"

"My sister's friend? Are you sure? That doesn't seem logical."

"I'm positive. There's no mistaking that hair, even from a distance. Hell, likely even from outer space! I'm sorry, Nathan. This certainly catapults them both to the top of the list as suspects, doesn't it?"

"If you're thinking of going to see her again, please don't, Mali. I don't think that would be wise unless I'm with you. Actually, it's probably best if you let Mrs. Knuedle handle it. I don't like this one bit."

I actually hadn't been thinking of going to see her, but now that he mentioned it, it seemed like a good idea.

"I hadn't even thought of it," I replied honestly, neglecting to offer a promise to abstain from going.

"I love you to the moon and back," he said huskily. "Be safe; I don't know what I'd do if anything happened to you. I'll be back in a few days."

After hanging up, I did what I do best when I'm stressed; I cleaned. It helps me organize my thoughts. Although the place was already immaculate, I made it even more so, scrubbing the dust off the baseboards, doing a load of laundry, scooping out the litter box, sweeping. By midnight, I finally ran out of steam, gave the cats a smelly treat, took my thyroid medication and crawled into bed, my mind finally quiet, and my body exhausted to the core.

By now, you all know me well enough to know that I was not up at the crack of dawn. I dragged my carcass out of bed shortly after 9:00 a.m. and brewed a pot of coffee.

Hummer hopped onto the table to inspect my beverage while the kitten jumped into my lap and settled down for a nap. That reminded me that the first thing on the agenda this morning was to bring this little fellow to the vet to have him checked. I wondered what they'd do in terms of vaccinations. What if he'd already been vaccinated recently, but had escaped his home? We'd have no way of knowing.

Another thought occurred to me: he likely lived in the area before coming to my home. What if he was already a patient at the local vet, and they recognized him? I would, of course, have to return him to his original owners.

By a stroke of luck, they had an opening if I could be there within the next half hour. As the vet was just a few minutes away, I quickly threw on some clothes, jammed my hair into a ponytail, slapped on some eyeliner and mascara and rushed out the door. Then, I rushed back inside, this time remembering to get the cat.

The sweet thing had suddenly turned into a moun-tain lion as I tried to wrestle him into the cat carrier, spreading all four limbs wide in an attempt to prevent insertion. I prevailed however, and we rushed out and huffed into the clinic with only a minute to spare.

"Who do we have here?" the receptionist cooed,

extending a finger into the cat carrier for the kitty to have a sniff.

"He doesn't have a name yet since I've only had him a few days. He's a stray, I think. He just wandered into my home one day. No one's come looking, but I figured I'd better have him checked. I'll keep him, of course, if no one claims him."

She lifted him out of the cage and snuggled him close to her chest. "Is that you, Bart? It sure looks like you." She beamed in my direction.

"This looks just like a rescue cat that we were fostering here at the clinic. He escaped a few days ago. Where do you live?" Sadly, I explained that I was just minutes away and he very easily could have walked the distance. Would I be losing my kitty?

"Well, we'll know soon enough if it's Bart. He has a chip implanted in him, so let's have a look." She scanned him and confirmed what I feared. It was Bart.

"It looks like he got tired of waiting for someone to adopt him and went out to find himself a real home. If you're interested in adopting him, we can fill out the paperwork today. The adoption fee is $75.00, but the checkup is free, he's already been vaccinated, and he's scheduled to be fixed in a couple of weeks, also free of charge. After that, he's officially yours."

"Absolutely!" I exclaimed, breathing a sigh of relief. The kitty would be mine. I wasn't crazy about his name, but maybe it would grow on me.

20 minutes later, Bart had a clean bill of health, I was armed with kitten food (also included in the

$75.00 adoption fee), and we were back at home. Hummer trotted over to us, gave Bart a sniff, then made friends with the bag of kitten food, rubbing his scent all over it. I marvelled at his good nature until he did an about-face and hissed at Bart before tearing down the hallway, yowling.

I brewed more coffee and a few minutes later settled down with my notepad, reviewing the details of the case. I had to get back to Georgie's house to interview her, but today was out of the question as the bistro would be re-opening and I had work to do.

I headed downstairs to give it a thorough cleaning and burned peppermint essential oil in a diffuser to ensure that the smell of antiseptic no longer lingered. Then I set to work on preparing the evening's hot dish, which would be my mother's schnitzel with Greek lemon-herb roasted potatoes and glazed carrots.

Greek Lemon and Herb Roasted Potatoes

You didn't actually think I would divulge my mom's schnitzel recipe, did you? Even if I did, it wouldn't turn out like hers. I've tried many times and even though I follow the very easy recipe religiously and have helped her make it hundreds of times, if I do it on my own, it never turns out as succulent as hers. The magic, I think, comes from her meaty hands.

These potatoes, however, will not let you down.

- 7-8 medium-large potatoes, peeled
- 8 cloves of garlic, halved
- ¼ cup mild tasting olive oil
- ¼ cup melted butter or margarine
- 1 heaping teaspoon yellow mustard
- 5 tablespoons lemon or lime juice
- 1 teaspoon of each: dried oregano, dried or fresh parsley, garlic powder
- ½ teaspoon dried dill weed (optional)
- 1 tablespoon dried or fresh chopped cilantro (optional)
- Salt and pepper to taste

Preheat oven to 375 degrees.

Cut the peeled potatoes into wedges: cut in half, then cut those halves in half.

In a bowl, combine all the other ingredients except

for the cloves of garlic and cilantro.

Add potatoes and toss well so that it is all coated. Place in a baking dish (I use a medium sized glass lasagna baking dish) and cover tightly with foil.

Bake for 30 minutes then add cloves of garlic. If you add them sooner, they often burn. Cover with foil again and bake another 15 minutes, then remove foil and bake another 15-20 minutes until nicely browned. If the wedges are very thick, leave covered with foil for 20-25 minutes before uncovering.

When done, add cilantro and serve. Also great with a sprinkling of tangy, freshly-grated parmesan.

Chapter Eleven

My mother was the first to arrive, proudly sporting our newest selection of work t-shirts that asked boldly, "Are you ready for a French Kiss?" French Kiss was a wine, of course, stemming from the Sandbanks Winery in Ontario.

Before I could give her a hug and a kiss, my brother waltzed in after her.

"Sis, you shaved, looks great. I was thinking about spending the night so we can hang out?"

I seethed. "I do not have a moustache, for the thousandth time!" He cackled at me in return.

"I have two cats now; I'm not sure you'll want to stay," I replied, calming down. While I was mildly allergic to cats, his allergies were horrid. Surely this would dissuade him?

"It's only for one night. I'll live. I brought allergy pills with me. So, I'll go out and get my overnight bag." I bared my teeth in response, hoping it would pass for a polite smile, knowing it wouldn't, and somehow not really caring. In any case, his back had already turned. My grimace, however, was witnessed by my mother.

"You should be nice to Stephen. He just wants to spend time with you," she tsk-tsked me. She didn't know him the way I did, refusing to see his evil side. Or maybe she did, but turned a blind eye to it. He was always her favourite, and I don't think I ever really cared.

I mumbled something unintelligible. I wasn't even sure what I'd said or in what language. No matter, her attention was already focused on the schnitzels. My mouth watered involuntarily.

"How's your sink?" she asked, after a few minutes of working in silence. I looked at it suspiciously.

"What? Oh, yeah, my sink. Upstairs. Fine, fine. A friend stopped by today and fixed it."

Stephen was back with his enormous bag, stopped, grabbed a plate of salamis without asking, and then headed up the stairs, making himself at home like an unwanted bedbug. I'd deal with him later. For now, I had work to do. Murder or not, it was schnitzel night, so it was guaranteed to be busy.

All hands were on deck this evening: Nora, Nicole; then Chloé and Billy, who appeared to arrive together and were talking softly as they walked in. Could it be? Billy had certainly come a long way since he was back on his medication for schizophrenia and no one was happier than me. He'd saved my life, literally, a couple of times in the past and I wanted nothing more than for him to be healthy and happy. He'd had a crush on her for a while, and she needed a nice guy in her life. I smiled widely at them, but refrained from commenting.

If word of the murder had gotten out, it certainly didn't affect business, but again, it was schnitzel night. I was sure that I had record-breaking sales as the evening provided a steady stream of people and income.

Despite having a full staff, I still pitched in to help serve the tables. I was just rushing through the dining area laden with six plates of schnitzel when I heard my name. Well, my alias.

"Missy!" Only two people called me Missy and this one was the male.

"Milton! How nice to see you! I'll be right there." I delivered the six plates then returned to visit my unlikely friend.

Milton was a rich, doughy man with toad-like features. He wasn't particularly pleasant, had bad manners (or rather, a complete lack of), but somehow we'd grown close when his young wife had been poisoned at my bistro and we had worked together to help with the case. Although he was a frequent customer, it occurred to me that I'd not seen him lately.

"I heard about your recent adventures here; the lady wasn't poisoned, was she?" It was a strange attempt at humour, but that was Milton for you. Before I could answer, I heard my name again.

"Good evening, Missy."

Mrs. Knuedle! Oh, no! She and Milton were not friends. In fact, they'd been neighbours for a while and did not get along. He insisted that her dog was constantly crapping on his lawn.

"You!" he exclaimed.

"You!" she exclaimed.

"You!" Mr. Leonardo and I both exclaimed.

I was the first to recover. "What are you doing in here?" I looked about wildly. What could I throw at him? If I wasn't allowed in his pizza place, he certainly would not be allowed in my bistro, would he? "Get out!" I growled quietly so as not to cause a scene.

"Relax, Missy; he's with me. He'll behave, I promise." Mrs. Knuedle cooed. I relented, as I was indebted to her for her help at Alan's house, but I shot him a nasty glare.

"I don't really want to be here," he grumbled, clearly not happy with her. She ignored him, her eyes now fixated on Milton.

"Milton, you fat pig. I see you're still alive."

"I could say the same about you," he retorted. I quickly intervened.

"I have a lovely table for you, Mrs. Knuedle, at the other end of the room. Shall we?" I steered her away as she and Milton glared at each other. As if I didn't have enough on my mind, now I'd have to referee these two, worry about my brother upstairs, and keep an eye on old Leo. I glared at him as I seated them. "You owe me a pizza," I snarled quietly, "And don't steal my salami!" Then I smiled brightly for Mrs. Knuedle's benefit. "I'll give you a few minutes with the menu…"

"No need," she replied. "We'll have the schnitzel, with some red wine—perhaps a nice zinfandel...." I smiled at her, grimaced at him, and then returned quickly with two glasses of Boneshaker, which is exactly what I wanted to do to Leo. I grimaced again as I placed a glass in front of him then scurried away. I returned moments later with their meat, whispered a quick message into Mrs. Knuedle's ear to swing by the kitchen after her meal for an update on our case, then retreated again.

During the next hour, from across the room, I could periodically see her and Milton shooting each other scathing looks, but neither seemed inclined to leave any time soon. I was happy to see that Leo spent the entire time looking uncomfortable.

At one point, I slipped into the kitchen, retrieved the prize pepperoni that he'd thrown at me the previous evening, caught his eye, flashed it to him, then snickered my way back into the kitchen. Yes, I am childish. My mother raised a questioning eyebrow, having witnessed the tail end of my antics, but I just smiled.

Finally, Mrs. Knuedle poked her head into the kitchen and I updated her with my findings about Alan's girlfriend Georgina, Merri's supposed best friend. She glared at me.

"You stuck around after I left, didn't you? I should have guessed. That could have been dangerous for you. What are you going to do next?"

"No clue. I don't think I should see her again without Nathan, considering this latest news, but

I'd love another chance to speak to her. I'll think of something. I suppose you'll mention this to the cops back at the office…"

"I'm not back at the office for a few days. Just don't do something stupid." With that, she did something stupid–she headed straight for Milton's table, plopping down onto a chair directly across from him.

I watched in unconcealed horror as his mouth dropped. Even from a distance, I could see him stammer. I stole a peek at Leonardo, who also sat with his jaw agape. That I enjoyed, and momentarily toyed with the idea of sling-shotting a morsel of food into that opening.

A few minutes later, Mrs. Knuedle fetched Leo, and then they were on their way. I glared with all my might at his retreating back, to no avail. He didn't self-combust. Dejected, I waltzed over to Milton and plunked myself onto Mrs. Knuedle's vacated seat.

"What was that about?" I asked, point blank.

"I think…she asked me out."

"You think? What exactly did she say?"

"She said 'we should hang out sometime.'"

"And what did you answer?"

He started to laugh uncontrollably, until tears gathered in his eyes and the patrons around us shot us curious gazes.

"I asked if she had a noose!" He guffawed again. "A noose! Get it? Hang out, noose…" His laughter gently faded. "I suppose that wasn't very suave of me, was it?"

"It depends. Do you actually want to hang out with her? Like, not in a noose?"

"I hadn't ever thought of it. Certainly not, if she still has that crapping, yapping dog. If I had to think about it, though, she is rather spunky. Much older than what I would normally date, of course." Yes, she's your own age, I thought to myself.

"So, how did you leave it with her?"

"I don't think I said anything else, other than the noose remark. But she did natter something about stopping by one day. I can't imagine why; I'm sure we have nothing in common."

"What was her reaction to your noose remark?" I was curious.

"The old girl laughed, much to my surprise. I guess she thought it was funny." He puffed out his chest, looking quite proud of himself. I shuddered. Milton did fancy himself a ladies' man and had slept around with many of his younger staff members, but all of them had had a monetary incentive to do so. I don't think anyone, other than his deceased young wife, had actually thought he was handsome or had any sex appeal whatsoever.

Suddenly invigorated, he threw a few bills onto the table, thanked me for the lovely food and then practically floated out the door. I'd never seen him so chipper. It was quite grotesque, actually. I shook my head. It was unlike me to be so cruel. What was happening to me? Oh, yes: Stephen. His mere presence tainted my soul.

With the evening winding down, I left the bistro in Nicole's charge and trudged up the stairs to my living quarters. Stephen shrieked in horror as I suddenly emerged from the staircase into the kitchen. He'd had about half his body inside my pantry and hit his head on a shelf in surprise.

"What are you doing here?" he grumbled at me.

"Excuse me? I live here. What are you doing in my pantry? It's too small for you to move into, if that's what you're trying to do, with your body crammed in there like that." It was my way of saying he was fat, without actually saying he was fat.

"I was looking for some chips. Don't you have potato chips around here?"

I gasped. My weakness, and he knew it. "No, I don't. Chips and I can't be around each other. It's dangerous. I have crackers and home-made hummus, if you'd like, or more meat and cheese."

"Nah," he said, almost turning up his nose at my suggestions. "I'm going to shower now." With that, he marched into the bathroom.

Now, even for Stephen, his behaviour was extremely strange. First off, he was practically on the bottom of my pantry floor, looking in strange places for an elusive bag of chips. And he was showering at night. Stephen had always been a morning shower person.

Taking advantage of these few minutes while he'd be busy, I slunk into the spare bedroom and glanced about. He hadn't even opened his overnight bag, despite having been here three hours at this point.

Hearing the water running, I toed the bag. It felt almost empty. I snuck out to the hallway for a proper listen. Yes, the shower was still running, Stephen was humming. I snuck back into the room, quickly unzipped the bag and peered inside.

All he had inside was a pair of socks, a shirt, anti-perspirant and ugly underwear. Why the huge bag?

I heard the shower door opening, quickly zipped the bag, and then busied myself with the litter box that was in the room.

"Hey! What are you doing in here?" he practically barked at me.

"I'm taking the litter box out, unless you want me to leave it here for you to use?" I smiled sweetly despite being on high alert. He sure was jumpy, not at all like his normal, somewhat jovial self. What was he after? I thought of his comment about working two jobs. I knew in the past he'd engaged a bit too enthusiastically in gambling. Was he in trouble? Had he been searching my house, hoping to find money?

I hurried out of the room, relocated the litter box to a remote corner of the living room, showed the cats where it was, and then zipped into my bedroom. I rummaged way at the back of my closet and hauled out the heavy metal safety deposit box that I kept there inside a big cardboard box. Taking the decoy clothes off the top, I lifted out the steel box. It didn't appear to have been tampered with. I opened the combination lock and peered inside. While I didn't have much squirrelled away, there were a couple of gold chains I never wore, one thousand, five hundred dollars in cash (emergency money) and some weird bank notes or promissory type of something Hungarian that my parents had given to me as a memory of Hungary. They'd had them framed and used to have it displayed on their wall when they still lived in Montreal. Now that they had downsized and moved to Robin, they'd given them to me. I had promptly removed them from their ugly frames and slipped the notes into my safe, intending to research them one day. I wondered idly if these artifacts could possibly be the objects at the root of Steph's sudden interest? My parents claimed that they were worthless, but maybe Steph knew something that I didn't know. I made a mental note to research them tomorrow, and in the meantime I would try to pump him for information.

That, of course, did not exactly go according to plan.

Chapter Twelve

Relieved that nothing was amiss, I put the small safe back into the cardboard box and then placed the random clothing over the top, just as it had been before. As further incentive to stay away, I placed a couple of super-sized tampons directly on top. If anyone snooped, they'd have to deal with the tampons first.

I joined Stephen on the couch, smirking to myself as the two cats crowded him. He was clearly uncomfortable, which naturally made me happy.

"Can you get them away from me?" He sneezed three times consecutively amidst his question.

"It's best if you just let them sniff you, and then they'll lose interest. Otherwise they'll just keep coming back." He sneezed a dozen more times before both the cats settled several feet away from him. They apparently didn't trust him either. He seemed to be giving off a vibe I'd not felt before, even despite our numerous rough patches.

"Tell me, what's with the two jobs these days?"

"Well, one is part-time and the other one, they're downsizing. Lots of people have been laid-off recently, so anytime they're looking for someone to do over-time, I step up. I figure if I'm always there for them, maybe I won't get laid-off like the others."

"So, why aren't you there now?"

"I'd accumulated so much vacation time that they more or less made me take a couple of weeks off. Company policy. So, I figured this was the perfect time to visit you, and our parents, of course. I see you inherited a few things from them." He changed the subject, looking around my apartment with curiosity. He clearly wasn't comfortable talking about work and I suspected he'd already been laid off.

"Some Murano glass, a few old Pyrex casserole dishes and bowls—nothing you'd be interested in, surely. Mom said that you always referred to it as *old shit*."

He scoffed. "You can have that junk. You didn't want any of her framed stuff?"

He was slowly getting to what I suspected was the point. I played dumb, certain now that he was after those bank notes. "You mean, like her framed, hand-stitched, embroidered pictures? I've never been interested in those dust-traps. I told her that many years ago. She keeps saying when they pass away, they will all go to you." I let out an evil snicker, knowing he hated those pictures too.

"How about a drink?" I too was able to quickly change the subject.

"A beer would be great." I was disappointed, since

I had several wines I would have liked to have served him, such as Moustaches, in memory of how he always teases me, or a white Secret, for he was up to something. Definitely, a red Bastardo…

For now, I brought him a bottle of beer and mixed myself a cran-cherry gintini, with cranberry-cherry juice, pineapple juice, raspberry vodka, Bols liquor and Bombay gin. I needed something strong to put up with him, and the bluish-purple color soothed my nerves.

"That looks good," he commented, licking his lips and pushing his beer aside. He went to the kitchen to get a glass, taking his time, I noted. I imagined him going through my cupboards, looking for the elusive bank notes that were surely hidden between plates and cups, but I couldn't actually see him from the angle at which I was sitting. I waited patiently for him to join me, and when he returned he poured himself a healthy glassful from the big pitcher I'd prepared. Upon his first sip, his eyes bugged out in surprise.

"It's a half and half mix. Feel that nice burn?" I smiled sweetly again, enjoying his discomfort, knowing well that he had ulcers and horrid acid reflux.

"Good stuff," he gasped, unwilling to let me see that I'd won this round.

Emboldened by the strong drink, I took advantage of this slight upper hand and got right to the point. "What are you after, Stephen? You've been acting strangely and looking through my stuff. Is there something I have that you want? My God, are you the one that actually broke in here the other day?"

I blurted this sudden realization out loud, instantly regretting it as his eyes turned nasty. I'd not seen his mood switch so volatility since my teens, when we would fight like cats and dogs that were determined to kill each other.

"You can be a real bitch sometimes, you know that?" He spat the words at me with such venom that I was actually surprised. Sure, we didn't always get along or even like one another, but there had been times over the years that we'd actually been briefly close. What was his problem now?

I raised my brows, returning his glare in stony silence. I'd learned a thing or two from the cops, had practiced the brow raising and holding my tongue. I wasn't an easily intimidated little kid anymore, either.

He took another sip of his drink, grimaced, and then pushed it toward me. "What makes you think I've been looking through your stuff?" The nastiness was now gone, almost making me think I'd imagined it.

"Stephen, I am very precise with how I place my things. I'll notice even the slightest thing out of order, even a dust particle! So, tell me what you're after."

He sighed and tugged his salt and pepper goatee in frustration then ran his hands through his gelled hair. I was surprised his fingers didn't stick.

"Mom had said that she'd give me something, but she forgot what she did with it, so I just looked around. You don't have it, so don't worry about it. No big deal."

"What's so important?" I asked.

"It has historical value—part of our family history. It's just something I would have liked."

"Does it have monetary value?" I knew damn well that my brother didn't care about our family history.

"Maybe… I'm not sure. I was going to have it evaluated."

"It's those weird old banknotes, isn't it?" I couldn't resist. His eyes snapped to attention.

"Do you have them?" He tried to conceal his excitement, but I knew him too well.

I lied shamelessly. "No, I don't. But I remember seeing them at the old house. They had them in frames on the wall. I don't really remember the story—something about the government taking their family's land and giving them promissory notes or something?"

"They're called compensation notes, or tickets, in English. I can't remember what it was for, though, but I'm pretty sure that they have value. I think they're kind of like stocks or bonds or something like that."

"Are you in financial trouble, Stephen?"

"Of course not!" he lied. I knew he was lying, the way he fidgeted with his goatee.

"If you need money, I'm sure that Mom and Dad would give you some." My parents were very generous and wanted us kids to do well. My mother's wallet was particularly open for my brother, so I wasn't sure why he was so anxious.

He finally faced me, though he'd been avoiding my eyes during our entire conversation. I could see his anguish and ever so briefly felt sorry for him.

Whatever was going on, it was bad.

"I'm fine. Don't worry about it." His shoulders sagged, despite the brave face he was trying to show.

"Do you want to touch my moustache?" I joked feebly, eliciting a little snort of laughter from him.

"Aha! So, you admit you have one?" he joked back, and I liked him again, but only for a moment, and only because I knew we were both joking about a moustache. I touched my upper lip idly, out of habit.

For the rest of the evening, we remained civil and kept the conversation light-hearted. It was hard for me to hate him for long; I wasn't the kind of person to waste too much energy on hatred, and he could be very charismatic when he chose to be. For the moment, he chose to be, and even though I was almost positive that it was him who had broken into my home, I forgave him. But I wouldn't forget, and that is why I hadn't told him the truth about the compensation notes. Whatever trouble he was in, I was sure those notes wouldn't be worth enough to help him out, but my curiosity was certainly triggered. I'd have to spend a little time researching the notes in the near future.

Cran-Cherry Gintini, Toxique and Homemade Hummus

First, the drink. These are quite powerful, so it's best to sip it slowly and to have a little snack with it. Hummus with crackers or pita bread, or even plain corn or potato chips, are a great match.

- 2 ounces of each: raspberry vodka, Bombay Gin, Bols Blue liquor
- 4 ounces of pineapple juice
- 8 ounces cranberry-cherry juice

Mix in a pitcher or martini mixer, pour over ice and enjoy. If this is too strong, add more cran-cherry juice.

Toxique

Another of my favourites, with a gorgeous toxic green color, and not as strong as the gin-tini.

- 2 ounces raspberry vodka
- 6 ounces vitamin D fortified orange juice (get those vitamins!)
- Splash of Bols liquor

Pour all of the above over 4-5 ice cubes. Add more juice if too strong

Hummus

I recently bought a food processor so I've been going crazy chopping, shredding and pureeing everything.

I find that to make hummus at home, you really need a processor. I've tried other ways before and it just didn't work for me.

- 1 can of chick peas, drained and rinsed
- 1 clove of garlic, peeled
- 1 teaspoon chopped fresh cilantro (or about 1/4 teaspoon dried)
- 1 tablespoon chopped fresh parsley (or half a teaspoon dried)
- 1/2 teaspoon cumin
- A sprinkling of paprika (a shake or two from your spice jar)
- 2 tablespoons lemon or lime juice
- 2 tablespoons oil of your choice (I use olive oil, but you don't want to add that until the very end since food-processing olive oil can make it bitter)
- ¼ teaspoon salt, or more at the end to your taste

Place all except the oil in food processor and pulse in short bursts until smooth or the consistency you like. Add oil near the end and if the mixture is still too thick, add a bit of water (no more than a teaspoon at a time until it reaches the texture you like).

If you want to keep it super simple, use only the chickpeas, lemon/lime juice, salt, cumin, garlic and oil (and likely a bit of water until you reach the desired consistency).

Chapter Thirteen

To my great relief, Stephen left after breakfast the next morning, leaving me free to plan the rest of my day. I needed to talk to Georgina, but I also had to be crafty about it. I called Stella, thinking she might enjoy a little sleuthing. With her calm demeanour and subdued appearance, she'd make an unintimidating spy-mate. I was not disappointed. She arranged to finish work early and met me at the bistro shortly after noon. Thinking ahead, I also made sure that Nicole could arrive a bit early to open the bistro in case my sleuthing ran late.

"So here's what we're going to do," I outlined for Stella. "It might end up being a complete bust, but we'll wait for her to leave the house and then follow her. Depending on where she goes, I was hoping we could 'casually' bump into her and suggest going for coffee or something, whatever happens to be in the area. I already called her home earlier–blocking my number, of course–and she was home, so I don't think she's at work today. I assume she works, but come to think of it, I have no idea. Now, she might not leave the house. If that's the case, and if time is running out before I have to return to the bistro, then I may just have to knock on her door, though I was really hoping to avoid that. I don't want to tell you any more about this, since I want you acting completely natural. Ask anything you'd normally ask if you're meeting someone for the first time. Know what I mean?"

She nodded enthusiastically. We drove to Georgina's house, Stella chattering nervously the entire way. I was happy to see a car in the driveway and parked a few houses away on the street, where we could see her driveway clearly but wouldn't draw unnecessary attention to ourselves.

It was nearly three in the afternoon before the big bush of hair emerged from the house and headed to the car. I quickly started mine, ready for action. She made my job easy by heading in the same direction that my car was facing, so after several seconds, I eased onto the road and followed at a safe distance.

To my delight, she stopped at a Shawarma place with which I was familiar, good ol' Eli the drug dealer's joint. He was now behind bars, partially thanks to yours truly, and I had become a favourite here for some strange reason.

This was excellent luck, since I had realized that in my haste to start the stakeout I had neglected to eat. A rare occurrence, I assure you. We gave her a two-minute advantage before we headed inside.

"Amalia, pretty lady, so good to see you," the jovial Lebanese server called out from next to the sizzling meat that was rotating on the spit. "The usual for you?"

"Yes, please. Beef or chicken for you, Stella?"

"Beef, please, with plenty of garlic sauce!"

I could see she was practically drooling, as was I. In line just ahead of us stood Georgina, who, to my surprise, had not even turned her head to look our way.

"Georgie, is that you?" I exclaimed. Her hair whipped around in my direction. "It's me, Amalia. Nathan's girlfriend." Her eyes brightened in recognition, though she didn't appear to be pleased to see me.

"Oh, hello. How are you?" she mumbled, turning her head away just in case her flat voice wasn't indication enough that she didn't wish to speak to me.

I plodded on. "I'm fine. How nice to see you. How are you?"

"As good as can be expected." She glanced away nervously, eying her sandwich that was nearly ready. A flicker of annoyance crossed her face when the server handed Stella and I our sandwiches first. I paid quickly then purposely lingered while collecting napkins and straws for our drinks. As Georgina finished paying and moved away from the cash, I casually linked my arm through hers.

"Please, sit with us. It'll be so nice to get to know an old friend of Nathan's." She hesitated, but clearly couldn't think of a polite excuse to dislodge herself from my friendly death grip. I steered her to the table where Stella sat and introduced the two ladies.

"Have you been ill?" Stella asked, prompting a curious look from Georgie.

"Why do you ask? Do I look ill?" She fluffed her already fluffy hair.

"When Amalia had asked how you were, you said 'as good as can be expected'. I assumed you might have been sick." Stella smiled sweetly.

Georgie cast a look in my direction, unsure how to proceed.

"Georgie's friend is the lady who was murdered at my bistro," I explained to Stella, watching her eyes widen in surprise, then turned my attention back to Georgie. "As a matter of fact, Stella was there that night too."

Georgie squinted suspiciously. "Are you in the process of questioning her? Perhaps I should go."

"Not at all… We're friends. We're just out for lunch."

"Well, no offence, of course, but isn't everyone who was there that night a suspect? Isn't this some sort of conflict of interest?"

"Yes, almost everyone is a suspect, Georgie. I can assure you, however, that Stella is not under suspicion. She's actually Officer Sean's girlfriend. She had never even met Merri. You remember Sean, don't you?"

She paled visibly, clearly uncomfortable with this situation.

Stella quickly diffused the tension. "Are you here for an early dinner or a late lunch?"

"Both, I guess. I hadn't had lunch and I likely won't be hungry for dinner after I eat this."

"Is the other sandwich for Alan?" I inquired

innocently, noting the other wrapped, untouched Shawarma at her side.

"I beg your pardon?" She gasped at me.

"Alan? Merri's husband? Your boyfriend? Surely you remember your boyfriend," I chuckled softly, attempting to keep the conversation light. "How long have you been dating?"

"What in the world?" Words failed her and she stared at me, then quickly rewrapped the remainder of her uneaten food, scooped up the second sandwich and stood. She pointed the sandwich at me as if it were a weapon. "I… I have to go," she stammered, offering no further explanation before flinging her hair angrily then rushing toward the door.

"It was nice seeing you, Georgie. Take care!" I called after her. Stella and I looked at each other in confusion.

"That clearly didn't go well. I didn't even get a chance to ask her anything relevant, like how long they'd been dating, and if Merri knew. Well, she's clearly distressed that I know that she's dating Alan, so it's obvious that they're hiding something. Apparently, they want their relationship to be kept a secret. Which brings us back to the possibility of them being involved in the murder, right?"

"Is this what it's always like, trying to question people?"

"Sometimes," I replied. "I usually manage to get a bit further ahead, to be honest. Although I'm not a detective or a police officer, I do manage to get people to give me bits of information. She was completely spooked, though, which makes me even more determined to question her in more depth. Let's finish up, I have to get back to the bistro anyway, and I'm sure you have plans for a Friday night."

"Not until later. Sean is working until seven or eight this evening. But thanks for inviting me along; this was fun. Do you want me to keep this a secret from Sean?"

"Not at all," I snickered, imagining the look on his face and allowing myself a moment to relish it. Then I thought better of it. "But maybe just say that we got together for a late lunch and, by chance, ran into a suspect. I wouldn't want him to be mad at you, after all."

"Yes, that might be a good idea. That way, I wouldn't be lying, but he doesn't need to know all the details." She giggled, clearly enjoying herself.

We headed back to the bistro and she hung around for a glass of wine by the fireplace. I brought her a glass of white Accomplice, topped with some frozen green grapes. She giggled again. "Cool, because I was your accomplice today, right? I love it! And the frozen grapes, what a terrific idea!"

"The wine is on me. Thank you for taking time off work to help me." It was my turn to giggle. "Why don't you tell Sean to meet you here for a late dinner or drinks?"

She burst out laughing. "Hell, no! He'd kill me if I asked him to come here again. Not to mention he'd probably expect another dead body to turn up."

"Well, you have to know that he won't be happy we were out together," I said frankly.

"He'll get over that. I'm not about to have anyone dictate to me who my friends are going to be! Oh, my God; look, look, look, quick! Isn't that the hairy lady we just talked with today?"

I whirled around toward the door, and sure enough, there stood Georgie, scanning the bistro through her thick hair. Obviously, she could only be here to see me. I rushed toward her before she could change her mind.

"Georgie! I didn't expect to see you again so soon! Do you need a table?" I asked innocently.

"No, thank you. I just came by to apologize for leaving so suddenly. That was rude, I realize that probably didn't look very good for me. I was simply surprised that you knew about me and Alan. Listen, we started dating not long ago, to be honest, so we are trying to keep the relationship under wraps until we know if there is actually something between us. Nobody knows that we've been dating. I know that this must look terrible, but I swear we had nothing to do with Merri's death."

"Let's go into my office to talk there," I suggested gently, as the dinner rush was starting and people were beginning to arrive. I nodded to Nicole, indicating that I was heading to the back and that I'd be gone for about five minutes. She nodded in return, giving Georgie a curious glance.

Once inside my tiny office, I offered her a glass of wine, which she declined. I then proceeded to question her…gently.

"I understand that you might not have wanted your relationship to be public knowledge, but you must have realized that it would be discovered during the investigation, unless the two of you stayed completely away from each other. If you have nothing to hide, then it's best to simply be honest. How long have you been dating?"

"Only three weeks, I swear. What Nathan must think of us!" Her cheeks flushed with embarrassment. "We bumped into each other in the grocery store fairly late one evening and chatting led to going out for a drink. We had a very nice time and decided to get together again, for a real date. We've been together almost every day since then. Imagine our surprise when Merri just showed up out of the blue, after all these years. How did you find out about us?"

I ignored her question. "Did you tell Merri that you and Alan were dating?"

She shook her head. "No. I was going to tell her that night, at the end of the evening, once I knew how long she planned to stay. If she was going to be leaving again soon, I don't think I would have bothered to tell her. It's not like she really bothered to keep in touch, or tell me what was going on in her life. And to just leave Alan like that, without an explanation, or a goodbye…"

"Did she give any indication of why she'd returned? I know you said she wanted to make amends with the family, but do you think there might have been something else?"

"She'd mentioned tying up loose ends so that she, and everyone, could move on with their lives. And before you ask, yes, I knew that she was supposed to sign divorce papers with Alan. I think that was going to happen today, as a matter of fact. But that didn't have anything to do with me. He's been trying to get in touch with her for years and has been more than ready to put her behind him, even before I came along."

"Did you see Alan that night?"

"No. I was too afraid to go over there after Merri was murdered. Not afraid of Alan, of course, but I imagined the police following me there and immediately suspecting us of the murder. We had nothing to do with it, I swear."

"Do you know if Alan was there all night?"

"Absolutely! We sent SMS messages a couple of times during the evening. He knew I was with Merri and was curious to know how it was going, and if I'd told her about…"

"So, he knew that Merri was here that night?"

"No! Yes. I mean, yes, he knew, but no, he didn't have anything to do with it. I know what you must be thinking now. He had no reason to come here to see her. Everything was already arranged for her to sign the divorce papers. He wouldn't have wanted to mess that up by coming to see her and risk having her change her mind."

"You're certain she was going to sign the papers and Alan didn't just say that?"

"You're suggesting he set me up? I don't believe

that." Her voice turned flinty on me and I immediately softened my tone.

"Georgie, I had to ask, for your own protection. If he was involved, you could be in danger too."

"Impossible! Alan wouldn't harm anyone–especially not me. But not Merri, either, even after how horrid she was to him. He's just not like that."

I tried a different tactic. "Tell me about Merri. Did she share any information with you that evening? Has she been dating someone? What was she doing all those years? Why did she choose now to come back? There must be something that motivated her?"

"She was very evasive. She didn't say much about what she was doing for a living–*this and that, keeping busy*–is all she said. I did try to joke with her and suggested that there must be a man in her life. She blushed and admitted that there was someone, someone she'd actually known for quite a while."

"*Known for a while*? Do you think that meant it was someone local? Someone from her past…"

"I don't know. She wouldn't tell me anything else, but I doubt that it's anyone from here. I think she burned every bridge here."

"Maybe she kept in touch with someone we're not remembering."

"I hate to put Alan on the line, but he'd likely have a better idea about that. If you and Nathan talk to him, please don't tell him I suggested that you ask him about that."

"Of course not!" I suspected that she was unaware

of my prior visit to Alan's house and thought it best to keep it that way. He had, after all, thought that he was answering police questions that night.

"Georgie, how did you know that Merri was back in town?"

She pouted for a moment. "Can you believe it? All those years, best friends, and she doesn't even tell me. My brother saw her downtown and mentioned it to me, so I contacted her. I had to know. I was curious about why she chose to re-appear just when Alan and I began dating."

Out of questions, I thanked her for the information and escorted her to the door. Stella was on her way out and gave me a quick wave, and Hans was just on his way inside.

Oh, crap!

Chapter Fourteen

Hans–I mentally grimaced at his very name, only to discover that it wasn't all mental and I was grimacing in real life. On his arm was an extremely attractive blonde, almost the same shade of blonde as him, and just as exquisitely dressed as he normally dressed. I both pitied and disliked her immediately.

He gave me a superior sneer and, pretending not to know me, demanded a romantic table for two. I sneered sweetly in return and placed them at the table closest to the washrooms. When he demanded my finest wine, I raced back to the kitchen, poured some white grape juice into two lovely glasses, fancied it up with a few frozen grapes as I had with Stella's *real* glass of wine, then brought it back to their table before signalling for Nicole to take over. If he dared to complain, I would call him out right in front of his date, and he knew it.

Just when I thought the evening couldn't get any more bizarre, Milton and Mrs. Knuedle entered the bistro–together! I made my way to the door, wondering–nay, hoping–it was just a coincidence.

"Hello there, Missy," they both said together.

"Milton… Mrs. Knuedle… Uh, will that be one table or two? Is Mr. Leonardo joining you again?"

"I certainly hope not!" Mrs. Knuedle giggled as she placed her hand on Milton's arm. "One table will do, thank you. And you might want to pick your jaw up off the ground." She giggled again and Milton chortled.

No sooner had I seated them at the table closest to the fireplace that Stella had just vacated, when I could feel steely eyes grinding into my back. I whirled in Hans' direction, but he was captivated by the beauty that was with him. So why were my neck hairs standing on end?

I scanned the room and froze.

My father stared at me from across the room, his eyes filled with what seemed like hostility. I hurried to see him, my step slowing cautiously when I was a couple of feet away.

"Dad? Everything okay?" I stuttered in Hungarian.

"*Bazd meg*, Amalia. Is all yore fault." He spoke in English, his accent thick.

"What did I do now?"

"Bring me to table," he demanded. I indicated for him to follow me, my brow raised as I noted that his hobble was more pronounced than usual. "Should I carry you, Dad?"

He glared. "Is yore fault," he growled again, quickening his pace.

After he was seated, I brought him a glass of wine and a small plate of cheese. I plunked onto a seat across from him. "Okay, what's my fault? Out with it."

"The yoga is killing me. If I hadn't helped you with that case a few months ago, Mama wouldn't have forced me to go to this class with her."

I burst out laughing, gaining an even fiercer glare from him. Time for damage control…

"Dad, your help was valuable. I couldn't have done it without you, and I know that you enjoyed it too. Don't worry; the yoga will soon be over. You might even discover that you like it after a few more sessions."

This earned me yet another glare.

"Mr. Kis! How nice to see you! Looking good, looking good. I'd stay to chat but I have to get back to my beautiful date." Hans came and went before either of us could react.

"Vat the heck?" my dad finally exclaimed.

"That's Hans for you. Just ignore him. Listen, I have to get back to work. You sit and relax as long as you like."

I returned to the hustle and bustle of the bistro and happily alternated between serving tables and working in the kitchen. About an hour later, a commotion caught my ears, prompting me to rush out of the kitchen in a panic. Was Hans up to something? Did Alan come by to yell at me? Did a customer find one of my long, cinnamon-coloured hairs in their food?

"YOU! It's all your fault!" Mr. Leonardo barked from across the room, prompting every customer to turn in my direction.

"Oh, don't be silly, Leo. Sit down and hush up.

Milton and I just bumped into each other and decided to come for a bite to eat." Mrs. Knuedle tugged at his sleeve forcefully, giving him no choice but to sit at the table with her and Milton. Even from several feet away, I could see Milton sweating profusely.

As everyone in the bistro returned to their food, I indicated to Nicole to tend to Leo while I retreated to the kitchen. I had no intention of emerging until everyone was gone, with the way my luck was going. Unfortunately, that didn't mean people couldn't seek me out, which is exactly what Hans did.

"Hey!" He poked his head into my domain, my lair, my safe-haven. "Thanks for the great dinner and the wine. I'm leaving now. I probably won't be back; Stephania and I are moving to Toronto soon. It'll be much better for her modelling career there. So, I just wanted to say good-bye. I'm sorry things didn't work out between us but, damn, look what I've landed!"

And just like that, he was gone without even giving me a chance to say a word. Like a sloth, my jaw again dropped in slow motion, and I just stood there, cheese knife in one hand and the other clutching a piece of salami. Nicole found me in that position minutes later.

"Is he gone? Are they all gone?" I turned my eyes in her direction. "Please tell me that everyone I know out there is finally gone?"

"Everyone is gone," she replied gently, taking the knife from me then plucking the salami from my other hand and popping it into her mouth. "What is going on tonight, anyway?"

"Must be a full moon," I mumbled. "Can we close up early? Like now, for instance?"

"Just one couple left, so unless someone else walks in, we're good to go," she assured me. "I'll choose us a bottle of wine and start setting up our favourite spot. I'm sure they'll be gone soon."

Half an hour later, I flipped over the closed sign, closed the blinds, dimmed the lights and then sank gratefully onto the fake leather couch near the fire. I sipped mightily from the huge glass of Sunshine cabernet that Nicole had poured for me.

"Damn that's good. But why Sunshine? I feel anything but sunny."

"You were so gloomy by the end of the evening that it felt like a big, black cloud was hovering over you. Sunshine is exactly what you need!"

I couldn't argue with her logic. We drank in peace for a while before I filled her in on the night's events.

"Why do you think Hans even bothered coming here tonight?" she asked.

"Everything seems to be about closure these days," I replied. "He's found a beautiful model and is moving on. In his petty way, he thinks he's rubbing it in my face. Strangely enough, I don't think I'll see him again. Oh, don't worry, I won't miss him," I hurried to add in response to her glance. "Not in the least," I assured her.

"So, what's going on with the murder? Any news yet?"

I shook my head in frustration. "I feel as if things are moving slower than usual. Maybe it's because Nathan is involved—indirectly, of course—that I'm treading so lightly. But, you know, I'm growing tired of this. Tomorrow, I'm going to speak to his ex-brother-in-law again, and hopefully walk away with a list of people Merri used to hang out with. I have to start talking to more people, stir things up a little, get something done. I hate constantly having a cloud over my head, as you called it. It seems everything goes great for a short while, and then something happens. It's draining." I drained my glass with determination for emphasis.

"When is Nathan coming back?" Nicole asked cautiously, aware of the change in my mood but unsure how to interpret it.

"Tomorrow morning, which is exactly why I was hoping to talk to Alan later in the day."

"Can I assume you'll go with Nathan, then, and you don't need backup?"

I nodded. "Whether he likes it or not, we're going over there tomorrow, together. I'll have to disguise myself, of course, otherwise Alan will recognize me. Let's call it a night, shall we? I'd like to be well rested by the time Nathan gets here. I have a feeling it might take me a while to convince him, but I won't take no for an answer."

Chapter Fifteen

It did take a while. I stood my ground and refused to take no for an answer.

"This isn't how I planned to spend the day," Nathan grumbled.

I slipped my arms around him, nuzzling his ear. "I know, Lovey," I whispered. "I'm sorry, but I'm impatient. I want this solved. Normally by now, I would have spoken to a number of people, but I feel like I've been too cautious, because of you. And it's because of you that I want to get this solved, so I feel as though I'm caught in a vicious circle. Let's speak to Alan and see what we can unearth."

First, though, I had to buy a new wig. The ones I had would draw too much attention to me, which I didn't want. I just wanted to look boring, hum-drum, and not stand out in Alan's mind. If he looked at me too closely, he might recognize me from my previous visit, when I had pretended to be a cop.

I settled on a mousey brown, long-haired wig tied back in a ponytail, worn jeans, a simple white top and not even a stitch of make-up other than my usual lip balm. Nathan confirmed by phone that he would speak with us, then we were on our way.

I gave Nathan a series of questions to memorize, deciding that it would be best if he did most of the talking and I only spoke if it were absolutely necessary. During the ride there, we went over the questions one last time, without much success.

"I'm flustered trying to remember all this, Mali!" He ran his fingers through his curly hair. "And I need a haircut," he muttered under his breath.

"Some of these questions will come to you naturally during the conversation. Concentrate more on showing genuine concern, and maybe put a spin on things to make it look like concern for him, with a killer on the loose, since he was Merri's husband. If he's not involved, it could actually be a possibility, and one that hasn't occurred to him."

"Wow, that never occurred to me either. You're good at this, aren't you?" He beamed at me with admiration, and I must admit, I basked in the flattery. It was nice to be the object of such open admiration, something I had rarely experienced. It was certainly not something that I had known in my relationship with Hans, although he did compliment me on my sandwich-making abilities and claimed that I boiled water better than anyone he knew.

We stopped in Alan's driveway, and after a shaky breath, Nathan nodded. "I'm as ready as I'm going to be!" he said.

"Good to see you, Alan. How have you been all these years?" Nathan and Alan exchanged pleasantries and mutual condolences before introducing me. "This is my girlfriend, Amalia. Mali, this is Alan, Merri's husband."

I mumbled a "Nice to meet you," but went no further.

"You're not at all like Georgie's description," he commented. "I was expecting a long-haired, red-head." He looked at me closely, but to my relief, showed no sign of recognition.

"Maybe it was the lighting that made my hair look red," I offered. To my relief, Nathan came to the rescue.

"Ah, yes, Georgie… I heard about the two of you," he chuckled softly. "How's that working out?"

Alan's cheeks coloured slightly and he shifted his feet nervously. "She's quite the spitfire. Not at all what I'm used to–I guess opposites do attract. I'm sorry, Nathan, I hope it doesn't upset you, since she was Merri's friend. I had tried for years to get in touch with Merri for a divorce before Georgie and I even went on a date. I didn't date for years after Merri left."

Nathan waved away the apology. "No need to explain, Alan. I'm happy for you both. It's natural that you would eventually move on with your life. There's no harm in that."

"Thank goodness you feel that way," Alan gushed. "I was worried that that was why you were coming here, and that you would go off on me."

"You have my full blessing, old friend. I'm so sorry that we didn't keep in touch over the years. But I did want to ask some questions about when you and

Merri were together. I'm sure Georgie mentioned that Merri had been killed at Amalia's bistro–"

"I swear I had nothing to do with it!" Alan interrupted. "Our marriage was fine–or rather, I thought it was fine. Sure, she was at work for long hours, but she was a lawyer, right? They keep long hours. When we were together, everything seemed fine, and then she just vanished."

Nathan quickly intervened. "Alan, I just wanted to know who she hung out with back then, and who the both of you socialized with. Maybe it's an old acquaintance that's responsible for her death. She had to have come back here for a reason. Georgie mentioned something Merri had said about someone that she'd known for a while possibly being of interest to her. We–rather I–just thought that it might be someone from her past. Maybe an old boyfriend, or if you thought she might have had an affair while you were together, or a falling out with friends... something along those lines."

"She mostly hung out with Georgie. I'm sure she had lunch with clients at times, but she never bothered to mention business luncheons to me. Let me think: we didn't get together with friends often. Again, she was always working, including weekends. As you know, there were family functions she missed because of work." Nathan nodded, remembering.

"Yes, yes, you'd often come alone to our gatherings, offering apologies on her behalf. Go on," he urged.

"Well, there was the McAdams family next door,

but they moved away years ago, to Australia, I believe. Georgie, of course, would be here, or they'd meet for lunch, Giorgio and his girlfriend from time to time. You know, I haven't seen or heard from him in years. Come to think of it, we hadn't seen him for quite a while before Merri even left. Then…"

"Giorgio? As in Georgie's brother? You were friends?" This seemed to surprise Nathan. "I thought you didn't like him."

"I didn't at first. He was more Merri's friend, since she'd known him and Georgie well before her and I even met. I suppose that's why I never heard from him after Merri left, even though I thought we'd somewhat become friends."

I made a mental note for us to contact Giorgio and hid a grin when Nathan seemed to read my mind. "Would you happen to have his number?"

Alan shook his head. "I never had his number, to be honest. It was always Merri that would contact him. I'm sure Georgie has it, of course."

"I do recall her mentioning something about him," Nathan answered. "Who else?"

"The only other people were family and friends from work. There was Mark and his wife Linda–neither of whom Merri liked–and Jack, but he's nearing 70, if I'm not mistaken. They got along quite well, but I seriously doubt that there was a love connection there. He's got one foot in the grave, so to speak."

Nathan asked for everyone's contact information all the same, as I'd instructed him to do beforehand.

Never assume anyone, however unlikely, was innocent, I told myself.

"You're wasting your time," Alan muttered as he scribbled phone numbers.

"You mentioned that she was often at work, Alan. Did you believe her? I mean, she swindled so many people. If she was actually at work, you'd think she would have done the promised legal work for her clients rather than simply taking their money, not rendering the service, and then leaving. Did you notice any unusual activity in your bank account?"

"I thought of that a million times after she left," Alan admitted. "I would spend hours trying to remember if she had been acting differently those last few weeks before she left. Truth be told, by the time she'd get home, it was well past supper time. She normally either claimed to have already eaten, or had leftovers, then we'd watch some television together, or she'd brought work home. I usually went to bed before she did, yet she'd be out the door in the morning well before I was up. We didn't actually see all that much of each other, which of course would explain why we didn't have time to have many friends. As for the bank account, in all our years of marriage, we kept separate accounts. I'd pay for the mortgage and she'd pay the rest of the bills. It worked for us and seemed to even out."

"What did you do to fill the time?"

"I did the yard work, most of the chores inside the house, the majority of the cooking and laundry.

I'd often golf or watch sports on T.V. I kept busy. In fact, I didn't really mind most of the time. I could do as I pleased, when I pleased. It was lonely at first, but I got used to it."

"Was it like that your entire marriage?" I couldn't help but ask, morbid curiosity getting the better of me.

"Oh, no! Just in the last couple of years, as she became more successful. We were never big socialites, but we'd do things together. We'd cook together, or go to the movies, and we travelled together. I guess work just took over." He shrugged, looking sad. "But I always loved her, and I thought she loved me. Obviously, I was wrong."

Nathan and I exchanged an uncomfortable glance, both of us sensing the sudden sadness in the room. I cocked my head in the direction of the front door.

"I'm so sorry, Alan. We'll leave you now. Thank you for talking to us."

"Why in the world are you involving yourself like this, Nathan? Are you going to speak to these people yourself? I've spoken to the police a couple of times now, although I must admit, they didn't ask quite the same questions that you have asked." He started to chuckle. "I had one officer in training here with a pepperoni sticking out of her pocket. Can you believe it?"

My eyes widened in horror and Nathan shot a quick glance in my direction. "You don't say? How bizarre!" He forced a shrill laugh. "Yes, I was actually planning on speaking to these people. As you yourself said, the police didn't ask the same questions we asked. You never know what you might stumble upon, right? Keep in touch, will you?"

We safely made it back into Nathan's Jeep before he burst out laughing. "It was you, wasn't it? With the pepperoni?"

I grinned. "There's a story behind it, of course. Mr. Leonardo had just thrown it at me."

"The pizza guy?"

In my haste to explain, I had forgotten that Nathan didn't know about our feud. Now I had to tell him. "Mr. Leonardo hates me. He has from day one, for the mere reason that I am his only competition. I also have reason to believe that he had an affair with the former owners' wife, Harriet, and holds a grudge against me because I'm the new owner of the bistro. Oh, and then, of course, Nora was dating him for a while, and when they broke up, he found out she works for me, so of course he thinks that I'm some-how involved in their breakup. Apparently, he has a very hairy back. Anyway, if I even set foot inside his pizzeria, he throws a pepperoni sausage at me. It's actually come in handy, truth be told, when I've run out of pepperoni at the bistro. The other night, when I went to speak to Alan on my own, Leo had just delivered a pizza, so when he saw me, he reached inside his car, pulled out a baton of pepperoni, and threw it at me. Right there in the driveway! Mrs. Knuedle was with him—remember, she's a cop— and she ended up being my backup. I didn't know what to do with the damn pepperoni so I just shoved it inside my pocket and hoped that it would look like a gun, but I guess the top of it peeked out and Alan saw it."

I finally finished blurting out my story, then risked a glance at Nathan as I gasped for air. Tears were streaming down his face as he laughed soundlessly. "Pepperoni!" he finally gasped out, wiping tears from his eyes. "Oh, my God, I love you!" he rasped, finally getting his laughter under control.

I shrugged, not sure if I should be offended by the laugh he'd had at my expense, or if I should feel warmed by his declaration of love. "Okay," I replied, shrugging again and causing another fit of laughter.

By the time he'd regained his composure, we were back at my place. He quickly called Georgie, who had already heard from Alan and had Giorgio's number ready for us. Luckily for us, he was home and agreed to speak to Nathan after some gentle convincing. The other numbers that Alan had provided were out of service, except for one-foot-in-the-grave Jack's. Nathan left a message, and then we headed immediately to Giorgio's home.

Chapter Sixteen

The route was one that was very familiar to me. As luck would have it, he lived about a dozen houses away from Milton in a posh area along the Ottawa River which was composed mainly of mansions and houses in transition to becoming mansions. Only a very few small, old, neglected homes remained.

Giorgio's house was impressive, to say the least. It was about four times the size of my own, with a wrap-around veranda, three-car garage and what looked like a little guest house (which was also bigger than my home).

"What did you say Giorgio does for a living?" I asked Nathan, my eyes as round as cheeseballs.

"I haven't a clue. Back in the day when I knew him a little better, I think he was a bricklayer. I guess there's good money in masonry? I suppose he built the house himself."

"That could be true. However, even to be able to afford land in this area, one would have to have a significant amount of money," I mused out loud.

"Not to mention that this would have taken more than a few bricks, which also do not come cheap."

We rang the ornate doorbell, hearing the echo of the chimes from outside, joined by ferocious barking and snarling. I shot Nathan a look filled with panic, but he appeared to be unconcerned. Moments later, the door opened and I fought to stifle a giggle. Giorgio could have been Georgie's twin, with his shock of bushy hair and matching bushy eyebrows. The dog, which I imagined would be frothing and licking its chops at the thought of an unsuspecting dinner guest (or a guest as the main course of a tasty dinner), was a tiny, chubby thing that looked like it had a permanent grin. It ran straight to my crotch and sniffed happily, then trained its attention on Nathans' crotch. After introductions, we were welcomed inside, albeit, not warmly. Although Giorgio and Nathan had known each other for many years, they had never been close friends, and Giorgio was clearly uneasy about our visit.

"You have a lovely home," Nathan commented, attempting to put Giorgio at ease.

"Thanks. So, what's this about?" He came straight to the point, apparently uninterested in small talk. The bluntness flustered Nathan and he shot me a panicked look, suddenly unsure how to proceed.

"I'm the owner of the bistro where Merri was killed," I explained gently.

"Oh, so you two aren't, you know, together?" He looked at me with sudden interest, his bushy brows almost forming a question mark. I tried not to stare in fasciation so he wouldn't think it was my way of flirting.

"Yes, we are; I'm also Nathan's girlfriend. So, you can see how upsetting all this is to Nathan. Not only was his sister murdered, but it just happened to be at my bistro."

"My condolences, of course, but what does this have to do with me? No offence, Nate, but I haven't seen you or Merri, or even Georgie, in years. Why are you here now?"

I could see that his rudeness was starting to get under Nathan's skin. He clenched his jaw briefly before speaking.

"I'm sure you know that no one in the family heard from Merri after she disappeared years ago. It's a mystery to us as to why she was back now, why she defrauded people back then, and why she was killed. We're just looking for any type of clue that might help us figure this out. When we spoke with Alan, he mentioned that you used to hang out together. We were just curious if you'd noticed any changes in Merri before she left Ottawa, if you knew what she'd been up to, perhaps knew who she was in contact with that Alan might not know about. Really, any type of clue that might help us put some of the puzzle pieces together and lead us to her killer."

"Yeah, okay, I get that. But why don't you just let the police do their job?"

"Fair question. Tell me, Giorgio, have the police talked to you?"

"Me? No! Why would they want to talk to me?"

"Exactly!" Nathan replied. "They wouldn't have seen a reason to talk to you, or even know that you used to go over to Merri and Alan's house, because he never thought to mention it to them. It probably wouldn't even interest them, right? So, you see, if we investigate things at our end, we might be able to find out something that the cops wouldn't know about, and it might help solve the murder."

"Sometimes, all it takes is one small, seemingly irrelevant detail to just blow a case wide open," I interjected.

Giorgio was silent for a moment as he mulled over his response.

Nathan continued: "Now, let's say it was your sister, Georgie. Wouldn't you want to get to the bottom of things and help in any way you could?"

Giorgio shrugged. "Not really. We aren't close, you know? I'd just let the police do their work."

"Well, Merri and I, and the whole family, were close, and we were all deeply hurt and confused when she disappeared. Apparently, she may have come back to make amends with us, but now we'll never know."

Giorgio quickly cut him off: "Knowing Merri, I doubt it. I mean, she was pretty self-absorbed."

"Are you saying she thought only of herself, or did she seem pre-occupied when you'd get together?"

"Both," he replied.

"What gave you that impression?" I prodded, hoping I'd get a clearer answer.

"She was stuck up, you know? Now that I think about it, I actually liked Alan better than I liked her."

"So, how did you end up becoming friends, if you didn't really like her?" Nathan questioned.

"She was tight with a girl I was dating back then. They knew each other through yoga class or something like that. Pretty sure that's what it was."

"Yoga?" This was the first that Nathan had heard about any extracurricular interests that Merri may have had.

Giorgio shrugged. "Every Thursday, I think. Sometimes they'd hang out together afterward. We only dated for about a year though, maybe less. Yeah, probably way less. More like six months. Or maybe only three. Probably not long before Merri disappeared."

"What was her name? Would you still have her number?" Nathan prodded. He was becoming good at this.

Giorgio scrunched up his face. "Man, it's been years... Shareese? Charlene? Sharon, that's it! No clue what her last name was. I doubt I still have her number–I've changed cell phones three or four times over the past few years." All the same, he scrolled through his phone. "Sorry, no Sharon listed in my contacts. Maybe Alan has it."

"Why would Alan have it?" I burst out before I could help myself.

"Well, because he was Merri's husband. Maybe he kept in touch with Sharon. They seemed to get along pretty well whenever we'd go over there. It's just a thought."

"We'll be sure to ask him. Thank you, Giorgio. I

have to ask: did Merri swindle you out of any money like she did with so many others?"

Giorgio laughed. "Look around you, Nathan. Do I look like I've been swindled out of money?"

"I suppose not," Nathan replied. "Are you still doing masonry?"

"I own my own company now, have for years. I let the others do the dirty work while I look after the office and getting new clients." He studied his manicured fingernails with a sense of pride, his eyebrows turning into happy smiles on his forehead.

Nathan congratulated him on his good fortune and the two made small talk for a few moments. With Giorgio having nothing further to contribute to the reason for Merri's disappearance, nor her reappearance, we soon took our leave, no further ahead.

Back in the car, we discussed the visit.

"He sure didn't seem to care for Merri much, did he?" I commented.

"That surprised me," Nathan replied. "I seem to remember something about them having dated for a while back in high school."

"Oh?" I exclaimed, suddenly interested. "Why didn't you mention this sooner?"

"I just remembered. It was when he first scrunched up those eyebrows in his weird way that it jogged my memory—a flashback of him at my house. I don't think it was very serious, and I don't think they dated for long. You know, a year, six months, maybe three," he replied, poking fun at the way Giorgio had answered our question. "He probably thought she was self-absorbed back then, too!"

"You know we have to speak to Alan again about Sharon and Merri having attended yoga classes. He never indicated that she had any interests other than work. I wonder if he even knew she went to yoga class," I mused aloud. "Or, maybe he knew and purposely kept it from us, to make it seem like she had no other interests and to prevent us from following up on any leads. But why would he do that, unless he had something to hide…"

Nathan interrupted my rambling. "Can we do that tomorrow, Mali? I'm exhausted. I'm not used to this kind of stuff. I don't know how you do it, but I'm drained. How about we pick up a pizza then call it a day?"

"Ah, there might be a problem with that… Mr. Leonardo has figured out that we're dating, so chances are that you, too, are now banned from his restaurant." I gave him sad, puppy dog eyes to lessen the blow.

"Banned? Me? I've been going there for years, Mali! How does he know we're dating?"

"I think your name may have slipped into conversations. Listen, he's been coming to the bistro with Mrs. Knuedle, so maybe there's hope. Let's go in together and see what happens."

No sooner had we set foot in the pizza joint when his angry face appeared from the kitchen, just beyond the cash register. "You! It's always your fault!"

I waited for some pepperoni to come sailing my way, but there was no meat forthcoming. I approached slowly. "What's my fault this time, Mr. Leonardo?"

"First Harriet. Then my lovely vixen, Nora. And now my beloved Charlotte. They all leave me because of you. Why do you do this to me? Why?"

"I have nothing to do with any of that! Harriet was married and left because they sold the bistro to me. I'm pretty sure I saw you together downtown shortly after that, so you were still dating; therefore, surely, you can't blame me. And Nora was also married and decided to reconcile with her husband. And I don't even know a Charlotte…does Mrs. Knuedle know about her? Have you been cheating on Mrs. Knuedle, too?"

"Charlotte *is* Mrs. Knuedle," he growled through clenched, yellow teeth.

"Well, she's clearly lost her mind, because she also dated Milton and she used to hate him. There is no way that you can blame me for any of this."

Nathan approached Mr. Leonardo meekly. "I don't mean to interrupt, but is there any chance I could order a pizza. It's been a long day…"

"No, Mr. double meat, double cheese. No pizza. Out!" For the first time in our relationship, Nathan glared at me as we slunk out of the restaurant. Instinctively, I glanced behind to make sure a pepperoni wasn't coming my way. I was almost disappointed that there wasn't one in mid-air.

We drove one mile to my place in complete, uncomfortable silence. As we pulled into the parking lot, I cringed at the sight of my parents getting back into their car just as we were pulling up.

"Damn, another minute and we would have missed them and whatever they're here for," I grumbled. I just wasn't in the mood for Hungarian after the day we'd had, plus, my mom looked angry.

Chapter Seventeen

I was right. She fixed her glare on me. "You make Stephen go away. He very upset after he stay vit you. Vat you saying to him?"

I groaned. "Oh, Mother. I didn't make him go away. He was snooping through my place looking for something. To be honest, I think he's having money problems, and I think he's the one that broke into my place."

My mother gasped. "Not Stephen; he not doing that!"

"I know, Mother, he's your perfect child." I shot my dad a glance. He wasn't Stephen's natural father, so he tended to see him for what he was, whereas he could do no wrong in mother's eyes.

"Mama, calm down. I think Amalia might be right. Stephen has not been himself lately and he did mention that he's working two jobs. He seemed very pre-occupied during his visit. How much money did you give him?"

As we'd switched to Hungarian, and Nathan was already crabby and tired, he cocked his head toward the house, indicating he was going inside. He was too tired, hungry and irate with me to stick around and pretend to be polite. This wasn't the time for introductions, nor did my parents even glance in his direction. I nodded absently, waiting to hear my mother's answer.

"What? I did no such thing," my mother replied, indignant, then made a move to get back into the car.

"How much?" my dad barked, making us both jump.

"Just pocket money," she mumbled, making me feel sorry for her until she turned on me.

"Why would he break into your house? You have nothing. Why would you say such a terrible thing? Stephen is always so kind to you."

I seethed. Sure, it was one thing for me to say I had nothing, but to hear her say it was insulting. I choked back my anger and answered calmly, "He was interested in those framed bank notes that you gave me a while ago, but I couldn't remember where I'd put them. Dad, those were yours. Do you know if they have any value? I'm sure that is what Stephen was looking for. Whenever he was here, I could swear he was rooting through my stuff."

My mom stamped her foot. "I've heard enough. This is ridiculous. Let's go," she commanded my father. His eyebrows rose in surprise before he burst out laughing.

"How much money did you say you gave him?" he prodded. She clamped her lips, refusing to answer, then retreated into the car and slammed her door.

He turned his attention back to me and I watched her lower the window so that she could eavesdrop.

"They're worth nothing. It's a memento, nothing more. Years ago, they could be cashed in for a few thousand Hungarian Forint–of course that's very little in Canadian currency. They had a deadline for cashing them in though. My family just kept it as a keepsake, a little piece of history, but nothing of value. I can see why Stephen would be interested in them, though, if he is having money trouble."

"I suspect he may have lost his main job," I blurted out. Normally, I wouldn't rat him out, but considering recent events, I'd lost any sense of loyalty that I once had. "It's just a feeling I have; he didn't admit it or anything. I don't know if you know this, but he had a gambling problem a few years ago."

My mother slammed her hand on the dashboard, closed the window, and glared at me from inside the car. How dare I say such things about her precious child? She clearly didn't want to hear any more.

"Listen, Dad, I know he means everything to her. For the life of me, I can't understand why, but I got over it years ago. I really think Stephen's in trouble. I suspect he's gambling again and has gotten in over his head. It's just a hunch, so please don't mention that I said anything. I'm sure if he's desperate enough, he'll eventually go to you and Mom."

My father sighed and shook his head. I was morbidly happy to see that he didn't just do that when it came to me.

"Ah, Sacrament," my dad said, using the French religious swear word he'd picked up after living in Quebec for decades. "I better get your mother home before she tries to drive off herself," he joked, since she'd never shown an interest in learning how to drive, but knew she was likely mad enough to try it.

He got into the car and gave me a final wave before heading home. Fearing our first argument, I wasn't in a hurry to head upstairs to Nathan, so I went in through the bistro first and gathered some cheeses, salamis and bread, before going upstairs.

Nathan was lying on the couch, but opened an eye and stirred when he heard me approach.

"I'm sorry, Amalia; it's been a difficult day. I couldn't stand there and be polite and nod and smile while they jabbered in Hungarian and didn't even look my way."

"I understand, Nathan. They don't mean to be rude, it's just that English is so challenging for them, despite the amount of time they've lived in Canada." As I spoke, I opened the packages of food and spread out the contents on the coffee table, much to Hummer and Bart's delight.

"No, this is not kitty food; it's people food," I chided softly. I steered them toward their food bowls and gave them a cat treat to lessen the disappointment. Then I grabbed a couple of plates, two wine glasses and a bottle of red wine that was in the fridge and headed back to Nathan, who was fast asleep on the couch.

"How could you be asleep? I was only out of the

room for two minutes!" I exclaimed, fully expecting him to stir again. His only response was a soft snore.

"Oh, well, more for me," I grumbled, filling my plate and my glass. I had no issues drinking alone. I wasn't really alone anyway. I mean, Nathan was physically there, and the cats soon joined me again, each curling up next to my side for a nap.

The following day, Nathan's mood was back to its usual good humour. After a lazy breakfast, I ran about doing my errands in preparation for the bistro's evening meals while Nathan visited his parents and later called Alan to set up another meeting that afternoon. We regrouped in the early afternoon and headed over to Alan's house.

"It's a good thing I often work from home these days," Alan groused. "Not that I'm not happy to see you, but I do wish it wasn't under these circumstances."

"We won't take up much of your time, Alan. Thank you for accommodating us so graciously," Nathan replied jovially. "We met with Giorgio yesterday and an interesting little tidbit cropped up that we need to pick your brain about."

"Oh? Something interesting came out of that cretin's mouth?" Alan replied, looking intrigued.

"He mentioned that he'd never particularly liked Merri, and that he would come here because his girlfriend, Sharon, was friends with her. He seemed to think they'd met at yoga. Were you aware of that?" Nathan and I both watched Alan's reaction intensely.

"Yoga? No way," he replied without hesitation.

"Merri hated exercise."

"Yoga is more than just exercise. It's often very spiritual and the beginner classes often focus more on stretching and meditation," I began to explain, but Alan cut me off.

"No way. She scoffed at things like that, preferred to use her mind for legal matters. If she had any down time, she could be found reading a good mystery novel." He nodded at the bookcases behind us. "Half of those books are hers." A book called *Asiago and the Accomplice* caught my eye and my stomach growled.

"In any case, I know for a fact that Sherri didn't really get along with Merri. She used to come here because Merri and Giorgio were, in fact, friends. Sherri politely tolerated her."

"Sherri?" Nathan echoed. "I thought her name was Sharon. Are we talking about the same person?"

Alan had the good grace to blush. "Ah, it was indeed Sherri. She and Giorgio only dated a short time, therefore I didn't really get to know her then. I probably would have believed that she and Merri were friends from yoga—certainly, considering how Merri had left, I would have supposed that anything was possible; however, I did bump into Sherri a couple of years later. We got together a couple of times. She never mentioned having been in yoga and meeting Merri there, but she did mention how she didn't particularly care for her. So I'd say this yoga story is just that; a story."

"Why in the world would Giorgio lie to us about that?" Nathan mused out loud.

"It could be that he honestly didn't remember," I replied. "After all, he wasn't even sure how long he'd dated her, or what her name was."

"About three months," Alan replied without hesitation.

"You wouldn't, by any chance, still happen to have her number?" I asked without much hope.

"As a matter of fact, I do. We check in on each other from time to time. What she saw in Giorgio, I don't know. She's actually a very intelligent woman, and he's such a buffoon!" He scrolled through his phone and gave us Sherri's number.

"Why would Giorgio lie over something that was so easily investigated?" Nathan wondered once we were inside the car.

"He probably didn't count on Sherri and Alan having dated years later, and that Alan would actually have her number," I replied. "He likely figured it would be a dead end, and Alan wouldn't remember anything about her, especially after having given us a bogus name. But, what's he covering up? Why is this Sharon suddenly important enough to lie about? Did he not want us to know that he was friends with Merri?"

"Do you want to pop over and surprise him?" Nathan interrupted my train of thought.

I shook my head. "I have to get back to the bistro. I feel guilty for all the time I've spent away lately. Plus, my mom is supposed to work tonight, and the last time I saw her, things didn't end well. In any case, we probably won't get lucky and find him at home again until the weekend. Are you going back to work tomorrow? I'd like to spend a bit of time alone with you." I fluttered my eyelashes coyly.

"Sweetheart, by the time you're done working, I'll be fast asleep. Promise me you'll wake me up…"

He gave me a mind numbing kiss once we got out of the car. "I mean it, wake me up," he murmured. Then he headed upstairs to repack his overnight bag while I headed into the bistro with a big sigh. The next few hours apart felt like an eternity.

Chapter Eighteen

I knew my mother was still mad when she didn't show up for work. Unfortunately for me, people would still come to the bistro in anticipation of their schnitzel fix. I'd helped my mother make it a zillion times, so it's not that I didn't know what to do; I had just never done the final step of frying them. That was always her job.

It was a long process, seasoning, then dipping the pork cutlets into flour, egg, then a seasoned breadcrumb mixture. Yes, my friends, two layers of seasonings!

As if that weren't tiring enough, the frying was hot and greasy work. Just when I thought I was done, more requests would come in and I'd have to start all over again. To my relief, they turned out exactly like my mother's—perhaps even tastier, but maybe I was just biased after having put my sweat and tears into it. And that, my friends, would be a third layer of seasoning!

So, by the end of the night, I was hot and smelly. My hair was limp from the grease and my pores felt invaded. I jumped into the shower and washed everything twice, but the smell of fried schnitzel wouldn't leave my body. Needless to say, I did not wake Nathan for a night of passion but, rather quietly, slithered into bed so as not to wake him.

I was just drifting off to sleep when the cats tore into the room, jumped onto the bed, ran over me, then over Nathan, flew off, then ran back out. I wasn't sure who was chasing whom, but I was relieved that they seemed to be playing rather than fighting. Unfortunately, it woke Nathan.

"Baby, is it my imagination, or do you smell like meat?" He nibbled my ear, tasting, and then buried his nose in my hair, sniffing deeply and moaning passionately. "I must be dreaming. It's like you're a giant schnitzel! This is my every dream come true!" He turned on the light. "Okay, I'm not dreaming. But you do smell like schnitzel. Did you bring me some?" His eyes shone with anticipation.

"It's in the fridge."

"Why do you smell like you rolled around in them?" he asked cautiously, one foot already out of bed and onto the floor.

"Because I practically did! My mother didn't show up, so I was in charge of the schnitzel. I washed everything twice with soap and shampoo and conditioner—I even put the conditioner all over my body—then scented lotion, then body spray, and I just can't get rid of the smell!"

"Sorry about your mother. So what will you do now?" He was fully out of bed and pulled on a t-shirt.

I sighed deeply. "I guess I'll have to go over there and make up with her somehow. Although it's rare, she can hold a grudge. It would be a shame if our relationship was damaged because of my brother." I took a sniff of myself. "Plus, I just can't be in charge of the schnitzel! No wonder my mom's not too crazy about them. She never makes them anymore at home. Now I understand."

Nathan snickered as he left the room for his tasty snack. By the time he returned, I was sound asleep.

"Did you contact Sherri last night?" I asked Nathan the next morning.

"No, I thought I'd leave that to you; I figured she might offer more information to you, being female. That is, if she has any information. I'm not too hopeful. I did, however, try to get hold of Giorgio again. There was no answer on his cell phone, he doesn't have a land line, and his office told me he'd taken a few days off from work and would be out of town. I'm back here in three or four days, so it'll have to wait until then. He makes my skin crawl for some reason, and I don't want you dealing with him by yourself." He embraced me, sniffing my hair deeply. "I think the meat smell is gone," he commented casually, though I could feel his smile against my neck.

"Not another word about meat. In fact, there's a few pieces left in the fridge. Please, I beg you; take it all!"

"Gladly," he replied, packing them into a plastic

bag. "I'll probably have some in the car during the ride home. Will you be coming to see me prior to my return?" He looked at me hopefully.

"I'd love to but I don't think I'll be able to this time around. One of my tires seems to be making a funny sound so I need to find time to bring it in to a mechanic. I don't dare drive too far right now."

"Why didn't you mention it sooner? I could have had a look."

"We were pretty busy; it slipped my mind. In any case, you can take a quick look right now," I suggested, batting my eyelashes.

"I'd love to take a quick look," he murmured, kissing my neck and peering down my top.

"Not at me, silly, at my tire," I giggled then swatted him away.

"Alright, let's go. You can help me bring my bags down."

He left, carrying only his plastic bag filled with schnitzel. I glanced at the two backpacks by the door and shrugged. About to pick them up, the door swung open again. "Forgot my keys," he mumbled, then took the keys from the key hook by the door. Again he marched out, clutching the meat and the keys. I rolled my eyes, grabbed his bags and schlepped them down the stairs and across the parking lot to his jeep.

"Have you forgotten anything else?" I said, a little sharply.

"Oh, yes! You're right. I forgot my cell phone." With that he dashed off, returning a couple of minutes later with his phone in hand. By then I had loaded his bags into the trunk for him, wondering if he'd even think about his bags. "Hmmm," he muttered, circling my car. "Which tire was it?" I indicated the one on the front end of the driver's side.

"What kind of sound does it makes?" I rolled my eyes.

"Wommmp, wommmmp, wommmmp?" I asked rather than stated. How does one describe a sound?

He got down on the ground and inspected the tire from all angles. "Sorry, Mali, it looks fine to me. Please don't delay going to the mechanic, though."

He brushed himself off then embraced me in a warm hug. "I miss you already," I muttered into his shirt. Moments later he was gone. Through the sadness, though, I snickered and wondered if he had deliberately played dumb to get me to carry his bags, or if he'd truly forgotten about them.

Cheese Balls

All this excitement has made me hungry.

Would you believe that I was always intimidated by cheese balls? I've come face to face with them over the years, but never dared to try. In all honesty, I'm not sure why but it just didn't seem to appeal to me.

Then I saw some recipes and realized most things in a cheese ball were stuff I already loved. So, here's a recipe for the simplest kind of cheese balls, using your favourite ingredients.

- 1 block of cream cheese, whatever kind you like, room temperature
- 1 cup of grated hard cheese, your favourite kind (examples: old or sharp cheddar, mozzarella, marble, etc. Hard cheeses with a sharper taste tend to work better)
- 1 teaspoon garlic powder, 1 teaspoon dill, 1 teaspoon dried chives (or use 2 tablespoons of ranch mix powder or dried onion soup)
- A few shakes of black pepper and salt
- 1 teaspoon of any other dried or fresh herb you like
- 1 tablespoon finely chopped veggies of choice: red or green pepper, green onions, Spanish onion, etc. Or you can omit the veggies.
- ½ cup chopped or ground nuts for coating, if you so choose (I usually don't, but many people do)

- You can also add chopped meats to this, such as bacon or finely chopped salamis. If doing this, use 1-2 tablespoons.

Combine all of the above except the nuts, mixing by hand rather than an electric gadget. Once combined, shape into a ball. If rolling in nuts, place nuts in a bowl and roll the cheese ball around in the nuts to coat. I just like to coat mine with more grated cheese.

Place cheese ball in a small bowl and wrap with plastic wrap, ready for serving (or simply wrap the whole thing in plastic wrap). Refrigerate until ready to serve. Remove from fridge half hour before serving to give it time to soften up a bit and serve with crackers of choice.

Chapter Nineteen

The first thing on my list for the day was to try to contact Sherri. After coffee and time spent with Hummer and Bart, I was pretty sure that I would keep the kitten's given name as the two names together sounded good. To my delight, I found them snuggled up together on my bed. I forced some affection on them then let them return to their slumber until it was time to place a phone call.

The line was busy. I tapped my foot impatiently and tried a couple of more times.

I was in the process when my father's laugh surprised me. "Vat you doing?"

"Dad! You scared me. How did you get in?"

"The door wasn't locked. I rang the bell. I could hear voices inside, so I knew you were here and let myself inside. "

"Sorry, Dad, I must have been wrapped up in what I was doing. I'm working on a case and am frustrated over the phone line being busy. Obviously it's a landline. You caught me talking to myself." He just shrugged.

"Your mother," he started, then hesitated, unsure of how to continue, "says to tell you that she quits. Sorry."

"What the hell?" I exclaimed. "She's going to quit and stop talking to me just because I told the truth about Stephen? What is wrong with her?" I fumed. Most days, I could swallow the favouritism, but this time I'd had enough. Not to show up for work one day was one thing, but to quit without notice was another.

"What do *you* think, Dad? Tell me honestly."

He hemmed and hawed, choosing his words carefully. "I think you are probably right. As much as I hate to believe it, I do think he is capable of breaking into your place. I found out that your mother gave him five thousand dollars when he was last here. Five thousand! And she called that 'pocket money'. I didn't even know we had that kind of cash sitting around at the house. It would seem that your theory is correct, and he's having financial difficulty. More than likely he's gambling again, as you suggested."

"And let me guess," I finished for him, "Mom doesn't want to see the truth and thinks she's just giving him a 'loan' and that he's going through a rough time, right?"

"Something like that," my dad mumbled, clearly unhappy.

"Well, I guess there's nothing I can say or do to change her mind." I stuck out my chin and crossed my arms.

"Maybe you could just apologize…" His voice trailed off as I glared at him.

"For what, exactly? Telling the truth? That's

ludicrous. She'll just have to see for herself when he keeps asking for money, or if something happens to him because he's in over his head."

He sighed and shook his head, but didn't speak. Finally, he put a hand on my shoulder, muttered that he'd see me soon, and then let himself out. I immediately burst into frustrated tears.

"Get a grip," I commanded myself after a few minutes of crying. "She's quit, and she's determined to dote on Stephen, so I just have to deal with it." Speaking out loud made me feel more confident. "I'll fry the meat myself, or remove it from the menu. And she'll come around eventually, once she sees that I am telling the truth about Stephen."

Feeling slightly better, I dialed Sherri's number again and was surprised when it started to ring. When she answered, I quickly introduced myself, indicated that I was working on a case involving Merri's death and stated my reason for calling.

"My name came up?" She was startled and sounded appalled. "I barely knew that woman!"

"It came up only very briefly in conversation with Giorgio. I would like to meet with you for a few minutes, if I may, just to confirm some statements."

"Well, why can't you just ask me over the phone right now?"

I hesitated. There really was no reason, other than not being able to see someone's physical and facial reactions, which may be more telling than what they actually say. In this case, however, I was pretty sure she'd simply confirm my suspicions.

"I suppose that would be fine. Giorgio mentioned that the two of you would sometimes go over to Alan and Merri's. Is that correct?"

"Yes," she replied, and of course it was correct. Alan had confirmed it and this was just a nice, easy, warm-up question.

"And how many times a week, would you say, did the two of you meet at yoga?"

"Where? With whom? Alan? Giorgio?"

"At yoga classes with Merri?" I asked more specifically.

She burst out laughing. "We never went to yoga class together. I go to yoga, but I certainly wouldn't go with Merri."

"Did the two of you not meet at yoga and become friends?"

"No way!" she exclaimed. "She actually scoffed at me when I mentioned that I was into yoga, as if I were some flake. What makes you think we met there?"

"Giorgio said that that was how you met her, and that the two of you would go over to their place. Is that not true?"

"No. I would go to yoga three times a week, sometimes more, and I never saw her there. She and Giorgio were friends, and that's the only reason why we ever went over there. I never quite warmed up to her. She always seemed distant to me."

Finally, I'd gotten her talking and volunteering information.

"Was she not a nice person?" I prompted.

"Sure she was nice, in a formal and polite way that I couldn't stand. She seemed far more comfortable talking with Giorgio about mundane things like work. That woman wasn't ever relaxed. And her mind always seemed to be elsewhere."

"Did you ever hear her mention anything about friends?"

"I know she was friends with Giorgio's sister. She'd mentioned that when we were first introduced, as though it explained her connection to Giorgio and why he would want to visit her. The only other person I ever heard her mention was her receptionist, something to the effect of how she didn't think she could function without her."

All very juicy news. "How frequently did you go there?"

"I'd say we went there four or five times in the three months that we dated. And that was four times more than I wanted to go!"

"Did you meet any of Giorgio's other friends?"

"Now that you mention it, no. I'm not even sure he had other friends. I don't recall him mentioning other people. I never even met his sister. I asked him about that once, and he said that they weren't close."

"So, do you have any thoughts as to why he often wanted to go to Merri and Alan's house?"

"He had a crush on her. I'm sure of it. He didn't really seem to click with Alan or talk with him very much."

"Why did you and Giorgio break up?"

"We simply weren't well matched. I was physically

attracted to him at first, but there was nothing else there to hold my interest once the lust faded." I cringed, flashing back to the wooly brows.

"How did you and Alan get along?"

"We hit it off great. In fact, we ran into each other a few years later and dated for a while, after Merri's disappearance. He's a very sweet man."

"Why did things end with him?"

"I wanted more from the relationship than he did. I think, in a way, he was still waiting for Merri to return."

I suddenly felt sad for both of them. Unable to think of any other questions, I thanked her for her time.

I moped about for a while before dragging myself down to the bistro to prepare for the evening. Luckily, I would not have to make schnitzel, as it was not on the menu that day. To my horror, I did find a couple of more pieces in the fridge. I angrily shoved them aside while I hauled out the ingredients I needed for the day's hot dish. Later, when slicing the cheeses and salamis, I jabbed at the leftovers with a bat of Summer Sausage salami before bursting into laughter.

"What's so funny?" Billy asked as he entered through the back door.

"I'm just laughing over my own passive aggressiveness," I replied with a straight face.

"Are you okay?" He looked at me skeptically and then before I knew it, I was pouring my woes out to him.

"...and to top it all off, my mom just quit. Can you believe it? All because of my stupid brother! I'm sure he's the one that broke in here, but now she won't even speak to me and I'll have to do all the frying, and I hate frying!"

The last part of the sentence was mumbled out around a mouthful of food. I was surprised to see a half-eaten schnitzel in my hand, and had no clue how the offending article had gotten there. Billy, too, was happily munching on some and nodding his head politely as he listened to me.

"I can help you out, Miss Mali." He still hadn't grown accustomed to simply calling me by my first name. "I've watched your mom prepare the schnitzel dozens of times. I'm sure that I could do it."

I had no clue that Billy was so observant. "Okay. If you're sure, then we'll give it a try. Thank you, Billy." His smile warmed my heart.

He'd arrived early and took advantage of this rare moment alone with me. He expressed an interest in wanting to learn more about everything "behind the scenes," as he put it, so I decided to put him to work immediately. We worked quietly side by side, preparing the salamis and cheeses for easy plating and putting the final touches on the evening's hot dish, a Hungarian casserole with potatoes, hardboiled eggs, Hungarian sausage, sour cream and cheese. Yes, that might sound like a disgusting combination if you've never had it, but trust me, it's damn good.

"Hey, what did you mean about Stephen breaking in here?" he asked almost an hour later.

"Well, a few days ago, there was a break-in. Nothing looked disrupted or out of place down here in the bistro, but my apartment upstairs was a mess, though nothing was taken. I'm positive that it was him and that he didn't find what he wanted."

"Do you think he was looking for cash?"

"I don't think he knows that I keep cash upstairs, but I suppose that's possible."

———————

The next couple of days passed rather quietly, with no word from either my mom or dad. Giorgio was still out of town, so the case was stalled. I had even driven by both Georgie's and Alan's houses, just to snoop around, but other than a surprise glimpse of Sherri at Alan's house, all was quiet. Even after a call to Officer Lynette, I learned nothing new and got the impression that things had stalled with the police too.

Billy continued to come in early to help me with preparation and showed signs of becoming a decent cook. He surprised himself with his abilities and was thrilled when I showed him the entire schnitzel process. "But it's not schnitzel day," he stated, looking confused when I asked if he wanted to give it a try.

"You're right, but I bought a few pieces to show you the process and thought we could make it for the staff to nibble on tonight." His face lit up with excitement. I already knew that he was a quick learner in the kitchen, so I was not surprised when the final product turned out perfect.

Just as the last piece was frying, Nicole walked in, her nose sniffing the air.

"Billy made this?" she asked incredulously while happily munching on a piece. "It tastes just like your mom's!" She gave him a big hug as he beamed with pride.

Nora's reaction was no less jubilant, having caught the tail end of the conversation as she arrived. "You saved the day, Billy. I know Mali hates to do the frying. Now we won't have to remove it from the menu, or listen to her complain," she snickered in my direction.

"Alright, alright, enough making fun of me. Now, get out there and work," I teased back.

"Miss Mali, could I try working in the kitchen alone?" Billy asked. "You could help serve the customers and I'll see if I can handle things here?"

I smiled brightly at him, as though he were my own son who was growing up right before my eyes. In reality, he was maybe only eight or nine years younger but I still felt motherly toward him. "If you think you're ready, I'm willing to give it a try. Let me know if you need help."

I followed Nicole and Nora into the dining area and was surprised to see some tables were already occupied so soon after Nora had unlocked the doors. A scrawny hand shot up into the air and waved frantically at me.

"Well, well. The two of you haven't killed each other yet?" I couldn't resist asking Milton and Mrs. Knuedle.

"Not yet," Milton chuckled, his heavy jowls swaying merrily as he looked upon her with shining eyes.

"Oh my goodness!" I exclaimed, unable to stop myself. "You two are in love. How in the world…"

I broke off quickly, not wanting to offend or embarrass them.

"I know, Missy, I know," Mrs. Knuedle cackled. "I guess opposites can attract sometimes."

That's for sure, I thought to myself, remembering how opposite Milton's beautiful, young, deceased wife had been. Not for the first time, I wondered what women saw in him and resisted the urge to gag as he smiled his rather strange, toady smile at me.

"Can we order a bottle of something fun, Amalia darling? I'm feeling light hearted this evening," Milton's voice lilted as he spoke. I shook my head in amazement as I left their table in search of something fun and light hearted.

I knew just what to bring them. I went to the kitchen, noted that Billy looked calm and in control, and then continued on to my small office area at the back of the house. I had just received a shipment of some wines that I hadn't yet had a chance to unbox. Moments later, I headed to Milton's table, wine bottle and two glasses held up in victory. I presented the bottle with a flourish and was pleased by their reaction.

"I don't know how you do it, but you always find just the right wine."

I poured each a glass of Fun, a rose wine blend from California. Mrs. Knuedle smacked her lips in appreciation, oddly reminding me of Nora. I glanced at her, across the room serving other clients, and shook my head in amazement. Other than the length and cut of their hair, the two could have been identical twins. I don't know why I'd never noticed it before.

"How's your case coming along, Missy?" Mrs. Knuedle inquired.

I sighed in frustration. "It doesn't seem to be going anywhere right now. I'm starting to think that one of her former clients murdered her and I don't have access to those names, so there's nothing I can do. It does make the most sense. Every lead I've chased down has seemed to go nowhere. "

"It's not like you to give up easily. You know there's usually some small thing that's overlooked that ties everything together. Go over what you know again, and again, and you'll find it. But rest assured, if it is a former client, then the police will piece it together. It just takes time, and sometimes a bit of luck."

"Speaking of luck," Milton interrupted, "a toast to you, my dear. I'm so lucky to have met you. I don't know what I'd do without you. You have made me a better man." He covered Mrs. Knuedle's hand with his, his eyes soft and doe-like as he gazed at her.

"That's it!" I exclaimed. I leaned over and hugged them both fiercely in my excitement. It almost bordered on a choke-hold.

"You're right, Mrs. Knuedle, sometimes it just takes a bit of luck. *I don't know what I'd do without you!*"

She smiled brightly at my words, not realizing that I was simply repeating the words Milton had said and that this was my clue. "I'll send Nora or Nicole to take your orders in a few minutes. Enjoy your evening. I have to chase down a lead."

My conversation with Sherri had suddenly come to mind, a small tidbit she'd thrown my way that I'd filed away in my memory but neglected to give it further thought at the time.

She had mentioned that Merri had a receptionist that she couldn't function without.

Mom's Famous Schnitzels

Folks, you've earned it. You stuck with me through four books; you deserve this recipe.

Other than salt and pepper, my mother never actually used other spices, so the two layers of seasonings mentioned in chapter eighteen were my own addition over the years.

- 1 package of boneless, thin sliced pork cutlets (about 8 pieces of meat, although more is definitely better)
- 2 eggs, beaten, in a bowl big enough to dip the meat in
- 1 cup of flour, in a bowl big enough to dip the meat in
- 1 1/2 to 2 cups of breadcrumbs of your choice, in a bowl big enough to dip the meat in
- salt, pepper
- 1/3 teaspoon of garlic powder, paprika, dill weed, dried parsley (these are optional spices— the only necessity is salt and pepper)
- 1/2 cup or more olive oil or oil of your choice for frying—you might need more

Salt and pepper both sides of each piece of meat then set aside. To the breadcrumbs, add about 1/3 teaspoon of each spice and mix around to incorporate.

Arrange the bowls in this order: flour, egg, breadcrumbs.

Coat each piece of meat in the order above. Flour both sides, then shake off any excess. Next dip in the egg mixture, coating completely and allowing excess to drip off before putting into the breadcrumb bowl and coating completely. Pat firmly so that the breadcrumbs adhere well. When done, set aside on a plate until all of the meat has been prepared. I use a fork in one hand to lift the meat from each bowl and my other hand to coat in the flour and breadcrumbs. Your coating hand will be gross by the time you're done.

In a frying pan, add enough oil so that it covers the bottom and has enough in it to almost cover a piece of meat. Heat on medium or just very slightly higher for a few minutes before adding any meat. Once a breadcrumb added to the oil begins to sizzle, the temperature is right.

Fit as many pieces of meat that the pan can accommodate without crowding. Mine fits four to five pieces comfortably. Each side will take a few minutes to fry. Once you have a nice, golden or light brown colour, you can flip the meat to the other side and do the same. When ready, transfer to an oven safe dish lined with paper towel to absorb any oils. Keep the meat in a warmed but not hot oven until all of the meat is cooked.

Delicious served with rice or any type of potato that you like (mashed, baked, fried, potato salad, etc) and a side of Hungarian cucumber salad.

You're welcome, my friends.

Chapter Twenty

I sprinted back to my small office, glancing quickly at Billy along the way. He still seemed fine and I was thankful to shift some of the pressure of working in the kitchen onto his shoulders. He had come a long way from just learning how to pour wine and wipe countertops.

My hands trembled as I wrestled my cell phone from my back pocket. Why hadn't there been any mention of a receptionist before? I knew Merri ran her own business, but it had never occurred to me that she had staff. Surely, in a small practice, a fellow co-worker would know if something was amiss. I had to find and contact this receptionist.

"Alan!" I practically shouted when he answered the phone. "Alan, Alan, I'm so happy you answered." I knew I was gushing, but I couldn't control my excitement. "This is Amalia, Nathan's girlfriend."

"Oh? Okay. Hello." He faltered, not sure how to proceed.

"I'm sorry to bother you. I've been helping Nathan

with the investigation. I spoke to Sherri. Thank you again for giving us her number. She confirmed everything that you said about Merri in relation to the yoga. She also mentioned something about a receptionist. Did Merri have a receptionist working for her?"

I was greeted with silence. "Hello?" I asked tentatively.

"Yes, yes, I'm still here. I was lost in thought. It's very interesting that you ask that. She did have a receptionist, for many years, now that you mention it. Merri was quite close to Lexy. I had completely forgotten about her. She was Merri's right hand, so to speak, for a number of years. She kept things running smoothly, handled all the billing and collections and setting up Merri's appointments, and no doubt other tasks."

"Was Lexy still working for Merri when she disappeared?"

"No. She had moved away about a year or two prior, which is why it never occurred to me to mention her. I'm not sure of the exact timeframe. I recall Merri was quite upset at the time, but she never replaced her. She decided she could handle everything on her own and save money, not having to pay wages. We all know how that turned out, don't we?"

Yes, I knew. It had enabled her to accept payments for services that were never rendered, and not get caught by someone else balancing the books and setting up her appointments.

"Do you remember Lexy's last name? What can you tell me about her?"

"I'm sure if I think about it, her name will come to

me. She was very attractive: green eyes, dark, long hair, very vivacious, yet professional. She'd keep her hair in bun at work to prevent unwanted advances from clients. I'm not sure it worked; she was still gorgeous. Smith. That's it! How could I forget that last name?"

"Alan, do you know why she left and where she might have gone?"

"I'm not sure Merri ever told me. If I recall, Merri had been keeping longer hours than usual. It was then that she mentioned that she'd been running the business all by herself, hence the late hours. Ah, yes, yes, I think she said that Lexy had decided to move to western Canada to be closer to her family."

Something inside me tingled. Call it my latent Gypsy senses, but I knew I had just blundered onto a major clue. Merri, too, had been "out west" these past few years. Had she reconnected with Lexy? Was she still practicing law there, with Lexi as her right hand again? Or was there a deeper layer to this? My senses told me there was something more.

But how was Giorgio involved? He had to be, otherwise why the little white lies?

I felt loose ends starting to connect, ever so slightly. It was there, but I couldn't quite tie them together. But I felt it.

"How does this all tie in with Giorgio?" I mumbled out loud.

"Who?" Alan's voice rose an octave. "Why would this have anything to do with Giorgio?"

"I'm sorry, Alan, I was just thinking out loud. I was

wondering why he'd lied and given a wrong name for Sherri and why he said she and Merri were friends through yoga."

"He's an idiot," Alan said with disgust. "I saw the way he watched Merri. I asked her about that once but she just brushed it off, saying it was my imagination."

"He can't be a complete idiot; he does have his own company, after all, and a very impressive home."

"I don't understand how," Alan retorted. "I guess there's a lot more money in masonry that I thought."

We hung up with that question still looming. How indeed? I turned to the internet for answers.

The average annual salary for a mason was in the $50,000 area. The range was approximately $30,000 to upwards of $80,000 for a highly skilled, established mason. Giorgio was in his mid to late thirties, therefore possibly at the higher end of the pay scale. But even at that, would he have made enough to afford the property he was on, even if he built the house himself, and to own a company?

I knew who could answer my questions without raising any suspicions. I jotted down a few notes then gave Georgina a call.

"Didn't you just get off the phone with Alan?" she asked with a whine.

"Uh, perhaps. Oh no! I'm sorry. You're there with him, aren't you?" It was, after all, suppertime on a Saturday night. "I just have a few questions."

"Our pizza is getting cold. Not to mention, I've been on my feet all day, cutting hair." She was grumpy and likely hungry. I'd have to be quick.

"It's Leonardo's pizza, isn't it? I promise, this won't take two minutes." My mouth pooled with drool at the thought of Leo's forbidden pizza.

"Fine. What do you want now?"

"Nathan and I were thinking of having a house built for us, when he moves back to Ottawa," I started my spiel, the bullshit spewing forth from my lips with ease. "I thought it would be nice if we paid someone we actually knew to do it. I don't want to ask Giorgio directly. If we decide not to go with him, I don't want his feelings to be hurt. I was just curious if you could tell me how long he's been in business?"

I was greeted with dead air.

"You know we're not close, right?" She finally spoke. "I can't say for sure. Maybe five years? He's been working in this field since he got out of high school, but his own business, that hasn't been for long."

"So, you would say he's quite skilled then?"

"Yeah, well, I know he built his own house, so yeah."

"Do you know what his work ethic is like?"

"Nope," she mumbled around a mouthful of pizza.

"Is he good with people?"

"Nope." More chewing. She didn't even care if she was being rude, yet I could not blame her. I'd likely be the same if that pizza were in front of me.

"Has he ever had a serious girlfriend?"

I tried to sneak that by her, but it caught her attention. "What's that got to do with hiring him?" she asked sharply.

"Sorry, absolutely nothing. I was just thinking of my conversation with Alan earlier, when he mentioned that Giorgio would always be watching Merri."

"That's garbage. Sorry, honey," she crooned to Alan in the background. "He'd dated her in high school and all he'd ever say about her afterwards was that she was stuck up and thought she was better than him. If he had any interest in her as a grown-up, it was probably just to get some legal or business knowledge from her, to help him start up his own company. Listen, I'm really hungry, is there anything else?"

I thanked her quickly and apologized again, in true Canadian style, for interrupting her dinner, then rushed back down to the bistro. The better part of an hour had passed in what felt like minutes but I was relieved to see that everything was in order.

Billy looked up from his steam bath over the potato casseroles and grinned at me, announcing that he'd decided he was going to enroll in cooking school. "Don't worry," he rushed to add, "I'll still work here. Cooking school would be during the day. Maybe you'd even let me test some recipes here? I've sort of been thinking about this for a while and have several dishes already that I'd like to try." He looked at my shyly.

"That would be great! Wow, Billy, maybe we could even be open for more days then. It would just be too much for me if I did it all myself. We can definitely talk more about this later." Nora had just walked in with a large order.

"I was just about to come up and get you," she said

to me. "Stella and that cop are here, and your dad's out there drinking a glass of wine and looking kind of sad. I tried to cheer him up, but he just looked at me like I was crazy."

"Thanks for trying, Nora. He probably just didn't understand you. Is he alone?"

"Yes. Go join him, Mali; we can spare you a bit longer."

First I stopped at Stella's table for a quick hello. I must admit, I was enjoying the pained expression on Officer Sean's face. "I see you were able to convince Sean to come back here," I couldn't help joking. He refused to meet my eyes.

"I wasn't taking no for an answer. He'll have to get used to it now that you and I are friends, and since he and I have decided to move in together." She shared her news with a wide smile.

"Guess you'll have me on speed dial now," he mumbled, a weak attempt at humour, but an attempt nonetheless.

"Hopefully, I'll never have reason to call you again," I replied. "Haven't you just been dating for a couple of weeks?" I couldn't help but ask.

"Yes, I know, it seems crazy, doesn't it? But both our rental agreements are up for renewal in a couple of months, so we thought we'd give it a try. We get along great. Sometimes you just know, right?"

I told them how happy I was for them and then made my way over to my dad, trying to gage his mood. "Mom let you out?" I ribbed him gently.

"She told me to get out," he mumbled. "We got into an argument about your brother and the money she gave him. She accused me of taking sides with you and said we should be doing more to help Stephen! More than five thousand dollars–does she think we have money to burn?"

"Sorry, Dad. Stephen hasn't come back, has he?"

"No, but he calls her every night. Such a good son, she says, calling every day." He looked at me pointedly, as though implying I should do the same. My eyes narrowed and he quickly dropped his gaze.

"I'm sure it'll blow over eventually, Dad. Has Stephen 'borrowed' money in the past?"

"Yes, a number of times. But usually much smaller amounts, as far as I know, anyway. I never said anything before since it was smaller amounts. I also searched the house and found hundred dollar bills hidden in the strangest places. I didn't realize your mother was like that."

"Did you ask her about it?" I was intrigued. I wondered if my brother knew. Nah, he'd be over there all the time, searching the house.

"That's why she kicked me out, told me to mind my own business. It *is* my business! That's technically my money, since she's never worked here in Canada."

He had a point there.

"Dad, why don't you go up to my place for a while? You can watch TV and relax. The place is filling up, so I need to get back to work, but you can stay as long as you want."

He perked up a little.

"I suppose I might be able to find a good *Lawrence Welk Show*, or perhaps a *M.A.S.H.* rerun." He wobbled upright, blaming his bad knee and not the bottle of wine he'd already consumed, then continued up to my living quarters after patting my shoulder.

Two hours later, I found him and the cats asleep on my sofa, a half-consumed bottle of wine sitting on the coffee table next to them. I strongly suspected the cats hadn't drunk any. Smiling, I covered him with a blanket, tucked him in, turned out the lights and crawled into my own bed. I didn't know it, but I had an exciting day ahead of me.

Chapter Twenty-One

I awoke to the smell of freshly brewed coffee. A small thrill ran through me, thinking Nathan had come home to surprise me, before quickly remembering that my dad had slept on the couch. Slumped over a cup and a half-eaten piece of buttered toast, he raised bleak eyes in my direction as he heard me approach.

"Mom will come around; you'll see," I assured him

"I already have," she replied, emerging from the kitchen with a plate of toast for herself. My dad's eyes had not been bleak, they were guilty. I stood there, speechless until he burst out laughing.

"You look like you've seen a ghost, " he laughed.

"What are you doing here, Mom?"

"Having had a few hours to myself yesterday, I was able to think clearly about everything. When your dad didn't come home last night, I knew he'd slept here, so I thought I'd walk over and join him for breakfast. And apologize to both of you…" She said the last bit so softly that I thought I'd imagined it.

"Okay. But what prompted this?"

"Stephen called last night, asking for more money. I realized then that, whatever he's involved in, it can't be good. He's never asked for so much money before. I asked him to visit and tell us the truth about what's going on. I didn't say no to giving him the money," she said to my father, "but I also didn't say yes."

I could tell that my dad was about to say something, then thought better of it. "Finish your toast, Mama, I'd like to go home. Amalia, I am very allergic to your cats," he announced, changing the subject and giving them a disdainful look as they both rubbed up against his legs.

They were soon gone, and then I sat slumped over my coffee as my dad had been just minutes ago. Before leaving, my mom made it clear that she was still quitting the bistro, and though this saddened me, I knew that she had found it to be tiring and hated frying meat, just as I did. Logic aside, I was still sad, as working together had created a bond with her that I'd never had before.

Mulling over the events of the past few days, I revisited the conversation that I'd had with Sherri. Already in a melancholy mood, I again felt sad for both her and Alan, their relationship having ended because Alan was still waiting for Merri, years after her disappearance. Had he loved her that deeply? Or was it simply that he'd never had closure? This, of course, was something I would never dream of asking him. The information regarding Lexy, the receptionist, also loomed on my mind, as did my brother's financial predicament and the rift between my parents.

So I did what I always do when I'm down or stressed. I cleaned; vacuumed, dusted, swept and mopped until everything was sparkling. Then, with a sense of accomplishment, I brushed the gloom aside and quickly packed a bag.

Despite my previous intentions of not driving my car too much until I could get a mechanic to take a look at the noisy tire, I found myself en route to Nathan's place. I missed him and I had decided that my team could survive a Sunday without me, especially considering Billy's newfound cooking skills. Nathan was next scheduled to work on Monday night, so in the meantime, we'd have two days together.

He met me in the parking lot of his apartment complex, as anxious to see me as I was to see him. It had only been a few days, but I ached to be in his arms again, and to recharge my energy. As soon as I opened my car door and lugged myself into a standing position, he enveloped me with his arms.

"Let's get up to your apartment," I rasped, overtaken with a healthy dose of lust. As soon as the door closed behind us, I was in his arms again. In full embrace and with our lips firmly locked, we stumbled our way toward the bedroom but only got as far as the middle of the hallway.

"I missed you so much," he murmured out of the corner of his mouth.

"Mmmff…missed you…mmm…" I responded in the midst of unbuttoning his shirt as he was tugging my own over my head. "Ohhh!" Another mumble, as his lips landed in the hollow of my collarbone. His hands slipped beneath the waistband of my jeans, prompting more unintelligible sounds and then another "Ohhh!!!"

"I don't know what you're doing to me," I finally managed, "but you're making my rear end vibrate! I rather like it." He looked at me in confusion then burst out laughing as he drew my phone from my back pocket and handed it to me. I had set it to vibrate mode and could see from the display that Nora was trying to reach me.

"Nora, you have really bad timing!" It was not the first time I'd had to point that out to her.

"So you've said. Put your shirt back on, we need you back here at the bistro."

I sighed as I looked longingly at Nathan's bare chest. Then I glanced at my phone, suddenly panicked. How did she know I didn't have my shirt on? Satisfied that she had not figured out how to video call me and that it was a normal voice-only call, I drew a deep, calming breath.

"What's going on, Nora. Has something happened? I can't simply return; it's a two-hour drive."

"Billy's having a panic attack. The schnitzel isn't turning out the way it's supposed to. The breadcrumbs aren't sticking," she repeated what I could hear Billy saying in the background.

"Put Billy on the phone," I commanded. When he came on the line I said, "Billy, tell me how you have the bowls lined up."

"Egg, flour, breadcrumbs; just like you taught me," his voice trembled, the panic evident.

"No, Billy. It's flour, egg, breadcrumbs. Remember, salt and pepper the meat first, then dip it in the flour, then the egg, then the breadcrumbs."

"Oh, geez! Okay. Yes. I've got it, Miss Mali. I can do this. How long will you be gone?" I could still hear the panic in his voice, making me doubt my decision to take the night off.

"I'll be back tomorrow evening. Listen, if there are any issues, you can call me, okay? I know you can do this; you had everything under control yesterday. Just relax, take your time; people can wait a few minutes longer than usual if necessary."

I heard him take a deep, cleansing breath, as I had earlier. "Everything will be okay. You can count on me. What's this note you have here though, about a cheese fondue? I've never seen you make a cheese fondue?" The panic crept back into his voice again.

"Don't worry about that; it's just a note for myself, an idea I'd like to try. Put Nora back on the line, okay?"

"Nora, he'll be fine. It was just a small error, now fixed. Do me a favour, though, and check on him from time to time. If he seems to be panicking, remind him to slow down and he'll be fine."

"Will do, Mali." She snickered then hung up. Crisis averted, I turned my eyes back to Nathan and was disappointed to see that he'd buttoned his shirt. I put mine back on and joined him on the couch where he had a drink waiting for me.

"Yum, raspberry vodka with diet cola." I took a fortifying swallow then decided it was as good a time as any to fill him in on my current findings.

"I remember Lexy," Nathan said with a smile. I didn't particularly like that smile.

"You knew her?" I asked, surprised.

"Of course. Don't forget, Merri and I used to be close. I'd sometimes pop in at her office and take her to lunch, if she was available, or bring her lunch. She was a workaholic and wouldn't stop to eat otherwise."

"Are we talking about Merri or Lexy now?"

"Merri, silly. Is it my imagination or are you sounding jealous?"

"Not at all… Why would I be? Just because Lexy is drop-dead gorgeous, judging by Alan's description."

"She is indeed," Nathan teased. "But she wouldn't go out with me. Trust me, I almost asked her out."

"Almost? If you didn't ask her out, how do you know that she wouldn't have gone out with you?"

"I passed the idea by Merri first to see if she'd be okay with me asking Lexy out. She got quite huffy about it then informed me that Lexy preferred women. I guess maybe she was just possessive of her."

I digested this new information quietly, though my entire body was vibrating. I actually checked my pocket to make sure it wasn't my phone again. Satisfied that it wasn't, I had to nevertheless listen to what my body was trying to tell me. The key was starting to fit into the lock that would unravel this mystery, once opened.

"Nathan, we have to find Lexy. She's the key to all

this, I know it. What do you know about her moving out west?"

He shrugged. "Nothing. I didn't get to see much of Merri after that. She was always too busy at work to have lunch. She seemed a bit lost, now that I think back. I suppose she had to learn how to run the office, in Lexy's absence, rather than just give legal advice and do the necessary paperwork. I think Lexy even prepared a lot of the paperwork for her, and all she had to do was review it and sign it."

"Did Merri ever mention anything about Lexy having family out west?"

"I can't say she did, but even if she had, I'm not sure I'd remember. It's been a few years now, Mali."

"Do you think you can help me find her?"

He ran his hands through his curly hair. "I can't promise anything, but I can try. Do you think we can do that later though?" His index finger tugged at the bottom of my shirt then traced a path across my stomach. I drew in my breath sharply, tickled, but also suddenly tingly again.

"What do you have in mind?" I teased, marching my index and middle fingers over to him and tapping him on the leg.

He hooked a finger under my waistband, as he had earlier. "You know exactly what I have in mind," he teased, and then leaned in for a kiss, reminding me of the real reason why I'd come running to him.

Chapter Twenty-Two

After we were done reacquainting, we ordered a deluxe pizza with mushrooms, onions, green peppers, pepperoni, sausage and bacon. Feeling ravenous, I dug into my third piece without shame. I'd had pizza on my mind since my phone call with Georgie and had certainly worked up an appetite for it. At least Nathan had found a good pizzeria in Kingston.

"You know, this almost makes me want to move here. Almost," I reiterated, so that Nathan didn't take me too seriously. He had tried to coerce me to move again and I was afraid I might one day give in. With the sudden and unexpected freedom I had from the bistro, it had been weighing on my mind more heavily the past day or two.

"If I find Lexy for you, will you move in with me?" he joked, but he looked serious. For me, it was nice to know that he was finding our time apart as difficult as I was.

"I might be a little closer to considering it then," I quipped back.

"Let's get started on our search then!" He scrambled around then finally dug out his laptop from underneath a pile of clothes on a recliner and powered it up as I cringed. Having just left my apartment as neat as a pin, it was hard to ignore the mess in Nathan's apartment. This was one area we were not compatible and that I would have to consider seriously before committing fully to Nathan. "Typical guy," I muttered aloud to myself, still chewing pizza.

"What was that?"

"Nothing. Carry on with the search. I'll do the dishes." And tidy everything else, too, I thought to myself.

I grimaced as I entered the kitchen. The sink and counter were full of dirty dishes, mugs, glasses and utensils. I could count how many days he'd gone without washing them based on the number of coffee mugs there.

An hour and a half later, I had the apartment spotless, with all miscellaneous items where they belonged, furniture surfaces visible and tidy, floors gleaming. Nathan lifted his gaze from his laptop, noted the empty wine bottle on the coffee table in front of him, and got up to open another.

"Amalia? Where did everything go?" He was referring to his bare countertops which had earlier been covered with a selection of wine bottles, warm beer, liquor, shot glasses and the like.

"I may have tidied a little. Some things are now in the fridge, others are in the cabinet just below the coffee maker, and the glasses are in the cabinet where your other glasses are kept. I noticed that you have a wine rack, so all the wine bottles are now stored in it."

"How efficient," he replied dryly, returning to the living room with a bottle in hand. "I do have to say, I never realized how great this apartment could look! Thank you." He looked around the room in wonder.

"I have a surprise for you, too," he said, smugly. My knee-jerk reaction was to run, fearing he'd whip out an engagement ring, however, my fears were unwarranted.

"I think I found Lexy. I cannot believe how many Lexy Smith's there are in the world! I've spent all this time scouring the Internet, dating sites and various social media sites, looking for her. I can't believe how many people have a pet as their profile picture, so it was not possible to tell who it was at first glance."

Dating sites? I lifted a brow but didn't comment on his search methods. He showed me his laptop where the picture of a beautiful woman in her mid-thirties looked back at us, a lovely smile playing on her lips.

"She's stunning. Is that the Lexy we're looking for?" I was drawn to her mesmerizing green eyes.

"I believe it is. I haven't seen her in years, but those eyes just pull you in, don't they?"

"What do we do now?" I asked.

"We message her. Then we wait."

And wait we did, until the next day, when all hell broke loose.

Chapter Twenty-Three

"Did you hear from her?" I asked as soon as I woke. Nathan was already awake, no doubt messing the place up again.

"Not yet," he chuckled. "For all I know, it's an old account that she doesn't even check anymore. Let's just enjoy the day." To my surprise, he bestowed upon me a lovely mushroom and melted Swiss cheese omelet accompanied with toasted rye bread that had been lightly spread with garlic butter.

"Okay," I mumbled around a huge mouthful, "you're a keeper. That's it, my mind is made up."

He burst out laughing. "If I'd have known it would be so easy, I would have done this a long time ago! Move in with me," he said for the umpteenth time, gazing softly into my eyes.

"I'm not saying no, but I'm not saying yes either." I flinched. I sounded just like my mother. "I need a little more time for a few things to fall into place, okay?"

We spent the majority of the day exploring the city on our bikes, and I was thankful that I had left mine at his place during my previous visit there. The day was glorious and refreshing, surprisingly warm for late October. We stopped midway for a small picnic of French baguette, creamy brie, old cheddar with a subtle bite to it, smokey and spicy Hungarian salami and rounds of turkey kolbassa. Just enough to sustain us for the fifteen kilometre ride back to his place!

———————

Exhausted from the ride and fresh air, we fell onto the bed. Tired, sweaty, and sore, we fell asleep after setting an alarm so that Nathan wouldn't be late for work. An hour later, we were refreshed, though still sore. I pouted as he dressed for work and I readied myself for my two-hour drive home.

"Why the glum face, my darling?" He nuzzled me then poked at my lips to make me smile.

"I just hate leaving. Each time I go, it's like a part of me stays here with you. I know, I know, if I moved here, then we wouldn't be having this conversation." I exhaled a slow sigh.

I zipped my bag, ready for my departure. "I have to be on my way. I'll text you when I'm home. Let me know if you hear from Lexy, okay? I just know she's our key to everything."

I almost obeyed the speed limit on my drive back to Ottawa. I didn't want to press my luck and grimaced each time I hit a rough patch of road and my front tire made that *wooomp-woommp* sound. Once I even pulled over on the side of the highway, convinced that

I had a flat tire, but again, visibly, all four tires looked fine. "Just let me get back home safely," I muttered aloud. Luck, for once, was on my side.

The cats greeted me the same as they always did, by wrapping themselves around my ankles and tripping over each other and me. Then the stare. "Where's my wet food? You haven't forgotten, have you?" Hummer. Then the slow blink. "I love you. Feed me!"

Cats loved and fed, I finally settled down with an evening coffee, against my better judgement, to text Nathan that all was well. To my great excitement, he'd already texted, advising that he'd heard from Lexy and had forwarded me the email. It was brief, just a few lines expressing shock, sadness and condolences regarding Merri. She ended by saying that she was currently in Ottawa and would look him up. She had some information that he would likely find interesting.

To that he'd responded that he was out of town for a few days, but that his girlfriend was investigating Merri's death. He also mentioned that I owned a lovely bistro that she'd enjoy. Unfortunately, he didn't mention that I'd only be open again as of Wednesday. In any case, she hadn't responded so we had no way of knowing if she had even read his return message.

By now, it was nearing a rare early bedtime for me. Still exhausted and sore from the bike ride, I decided to take a hot bath then go to bed. I was up to my ears in bubbly water when I heard banging in the distance, then minutes later, frantic banging on my door. I shot up from the tub, covering my boobs with my hands in a panic, as if whoever was at the door could see me.

The banging continued and I bellowed "Just a minute!" as loud as I could. I heard a muffled response but couldn't make out the words. I quickly wrapped myself in a towel and ran to the door, still feeling very exposed and vulnerable. I peered out the peephole and was only slightly relieved to see what looked like a woman. A peephole often distorts people, so I couldn't make out any familiar features. I kept the chain on the door as I opened it cautiously.

"Please tell me you're Amalia," said the woman in front of me.

I'd no sooner confirmed my identity than she begged for me to let her inside. Not seeing any visible weapons, I released the chain lock and stepped aside. I already knew who she was, so there was no need to ask her name.

Chapter Twenty-Four

"Please have a seat while I get dressed," I said, already halfway down the small hallway. I jumped into some tights and a t-shirt and headed back to my unexpected guest with my trusty baseball bat in tow.

"I'm sorry to show up like this," she began, eying the bat. "I thought your bistro would be open, but then I panicked because I was afraid I'd been followed. There were no other cars in the parking lot, but I could have sworn I heard rustling noises. It was probably just animals, or my imagination, but it got the better of me." She finally finished speaking while moving her hands frantically as she spoke.

I smiled kindly. "Sometimes my imagination gets the better of me too, and your nervousness is rubbing off on me. Hence my bat, in case I have to bash any intruders over the head!" My senses tingling, I walked over to the door to put the chain lock back in place then peered out the windows.

I couldn't tell if it was my own feelings of unrest, or if I was picking up on hers, but I was relieved that everything looked to be in order outside. All the same, I made sure that the door leading down to the bistro was also firmly locked. Since there was a nice gentle breeze, I left the windows open; there was no worry about that, since we were on the second floor and there was no way for anyone to access those windows unless they were adept at scaling walls.

"Everything looks calm outside. No strange shadows. Can I get you a drink or a cup of coffee?" I followed her eyes to the half bottle of wine, still sitting on a tray on my coffee table. "I'll get a couple of glasses," I said as I moved toward the kitchen. I returned with two glasses and a small marble cheese stone with an assortment of cheeses and crackers. I'd not had an actual supper and now that I was fully awake, my stomach was growling.

"Oh, thank you," she gushed, reaching for the food. "I'm sorry, I only arrived yesterday and I've been visiting family and friends all day today, but never actually had a chance to eat. When I saw Nathan's email, I rushed over as quickly as I could, hoping I could meet you."

I reclined against the couch, observing her nervous movements as she spoke. Lexy was beautiful indeed, and filled with bustling energy. I was captivated by her, and could only imagine how Merri had felt, working with her every day!

She'd stopped speaking and was returning my curious gaze. "You never asked me my name," she stated. "Obviously, you know who I am." She giggled, still nervous but loosening up from the wine.

"Of course! I wouldn't have just let you inside, especially since I was standing there in a towel! I'm happy that you've come. I have questions that I think only you can answer."

She nodded, openly observing me now, and apparently feeling more comfortable. I suddenly became conscious of the fact that, in my haste, I had neglected to put on a bra. I casually tried to cross my arms across my chest while I sipped from my wine glass.

"I think you've already figured out a thing or two," she said slowly, knowingly. "This seems like a good place to start; you are correct, Merri and I were lovers."

I was not surprised. She had read my mind accurately, those startling eyes piercing into my private thoughts. I nodded my head, encouraging her to continue.

"Does Nathan know yet?" she asked softly.

"If he does, he didn't say so. Nor did Merri's husband."

"I meant about you."

"Me? No, no, no, no, no! Nooooo! And no. Sorry, but no!"

"Are you sure?" She scrutinized me closely. "I must be mistaken, I guess. Sorry."

"I'm pretty sure it's a no. Not that I've ever...I mean...no. Jesus, this is damn good wine, isn't it?" I topped off our glasses, willing my hands not to tremble. She'd shaken me with her question, made me doubt myself, but only for a moment. Her eyes were just so mesmerizing that it was easy to get lost in them, regardless of her sex. It's as though she'd cast a spell over me.

"Not that I'm against it in any way," I continued, now more calmly. "But no, I am not gay or bilingual…. er, I mean, bisexual. I am fully bilingual. Trilingual, actually, since I'm Hungarian." I was babbling now, no longer calm as she continued to study me.

Is that why I was hesitant to move in with Nathan? I shook my head to clear my thoughts. No, no, no. And no!

"I'm sorry, I'm rambling. You surprised me with your question. I mean, I do find you extremely captivating, and I'm sure this wonderful wine has something to do with the spell that seems to have come over me, but I am very much in love with Nathan."

She raised her glass slightly, in a small toast to my speech, a smile playing on her lips.

"Is it okay if I ask a few questions now about Merri?" I feigned regained control and switched into detective mode. I just had to avoid looking into her stunning eyes and I'd be fine.

She took a long swig of her wine then nodded, ready to begin. That enchanting light seemed to leave her eyes and I breathed a sigh of relief.

"I apologize if my questions seem indelicate, and please accept my condolences. I'm sure it was difficult, not having attended Merri's funeral?"

"I didn't dare, since I had left everything behind, so many years ago. If I showed up, everyone would have been confused by my presence, and announcing that we'd been life-partners hardly seemed appropriate at a funeral. So I stayed away. I was waiting for the police to contact me, but they never did. No one has ever made the connection between us. I guess we both slipped away so successfully that we could also disappear at any time, just as successfully, without any clues. I can see that was a mistake now. There were so many mistakes. Unlike her, though, I had a chance to visit my family." She sighed and reached for her wine glass again.

"Did you and Merri fall in love while you both still lived here in Ottawa?"

She nodded, yes.

"How long did it last before you moved away?"

"Almost two years," she replied without hesitation, anticipating my question.

I put down my glass, about to ask the question, the one that I knew would blow this case wide open, unless I was wrong, and then I'd be back to square one.

"Why did you leave? Did you and Merri break up? Or have a falling out?"

"We didn't break up. We were caught. One day, we'd both stayed at work late. What am I saying, we usually were at work quite late. That's probably what brought us together before we finally realized we had feelings for each other that went beyond friendship or curiosity. But on this day, we had finished everything early and kicked up our heels to celebrate with a bottle of wine and some take-out food." She stopped talking and smiled at the memory.

"We'd placed a blanket on the floor, picnic style, and had polished off the wine, so we'd lost our inhibitions and weren't being cautious. At that point, we had our clothes off and were in an embrace when we heard a click. I still have nightmares of that click. Before we could react, we heard several more clicks, rapid clicks. Clicks that would change everything. Forever!"

She stood and paced, picked up her glass, put it down again, and fidgeted with her hands before sitting down again.

"We had forgotten to lock the office door and hadn't heard him enter. We both grabbed our clothes, trying to cover up. It was too late, by then he'd already gotten several pictures of us with his cell phone. He blackmailed us–Merri, specifically–for the entire next year. I had nothing to lose; I was openly gay and had been out for a couple of years. But Merri wasn't ready to end her marriage to Alan, divide their assets, give him half her business, cause a scandal, and risk losing clients. She also wasn't ready to come out. Maybe she wasn't even fully ready to accept it…"

She shrugged, lost in thought.

I gripped the edge of the couch, anxious about my next question. Despite my jumbled emotions, I spoke softly. "Lexy…" Her eyes lifted to meet mine. "Who was it, Lexy? You know very well that it's likely Merri's murderer. That must be why you came back?"

She nodded as she got up from the couch and started to pace again. She drifted over to the windows and peered out, a crease briefly wrinkling her brow.

"You don't really look surprised by any of this," she commented slowly. "Maybe you've already figured everything out."

"I've thought about it non-stop. I've been involved in some cases before, so it tortures me, not being able to help Nathan when he and his family are in so much pain, with so many unanswered questions. It was Giorgio, wasn't it?" I couldn't wait any longer and blurted out the name.

"Yes." She continued to gaze out the window. But there was more to this story.

"I felt responsible for everything. The guilt consumed me. Rather than stand by her side while she was being blackmailed, I ran. I left town, disappeared on the other side of the country, barely keeping in touch with anyone. I went about my life quietly. I found a job as a paralegal, but I did not socialize, with either men or women. You see, I am 'bilingual.' I had dated Giorgio for a short time before I acknowledged to myself that I had feelings for Merri. I never told him, since he always seemed to have a chip on his shoulder where Merri was concerned. He hated the fact that I worked for her, even though the reason we'd met was because I worked for her. I couldn't quite decide if he hated her or secretly loved her and felt slighted because she'd dumped him back in high school."

"Do you think he suspected?"

"I don't know if he was smart enough, to be honest. He really is quite a simpleton. But we should have known better. He'd often stop by, asking both of us if we'd like to go out for a bite to eat, or finagling free legal advice from Merri about opening his own business. From what I hear, he was successful on that front, since he has his own business now."

My ears suddenly perked to attention. "What do you mean, from what you hear? From whom? Who have you been in touch with, Lexy?"

She suddenly looked nervous and unsure of herself. "It seemed like a good idea at the time. She had been Merri's best friend, after all."

"Georgia?" My voice shrilled a little, though I wasn't sure why. Maybe I still had the taste of our last conversation in my mouth, and let me tell you, it didn't taste like the pizza that she had been eating. There was something she'd said that had thrown me off, though I hadn't yet figured out why.

"Yes, Georgie. I didn't feel comfortable telling her anything, though. She didn't greet me very warmly when I saw her earlier today, even though the three of us women would sometimes hang out together. I had come prepared to tell her everything, knowing that she wasn't close with her brother, and hoping she'd relay everything to the police to avenge her best friend's death. I have a flight back to British Columbia booked for tomorrow, and I never plan to return here again, unless I hear that he's safely behind bars."

"Lexy, why not just end all this now and go to the police? He is Georgie's brother, after all. What made you think she'd turn him in?"

"I knew they never cared for each other as siblings.

Even a decade ago, they were indifferent toward each other. I thought there was a good chance that she'd do the right thing, but I just didn't get the right vibe to follow through. As for going to the police; it's my word against his, right? And it doesn't exactly prove that he killed her. So he'd still be a free man, and I wouldn't be allowed to leave town, and I'd always be looking over my shoulder, thinking that I would be next. Not for me. I'm going off the radar for a while, until I hear that Merri's murderer has been locked up. And then, I'm going to put all this behind me and start a new life."

Having been involved in cases before, I could see the logic in what she was saying. It would take the police a while to investigate bank records, to trace where Giorgio got his money, if it was even traceable. Even if they could prove that he blackmailed her, they'd then have to prove that he murdered her. With the lack of evidence to date, it was unlikely they'd be able to prove it and, as Lexy said, he'd be free to strike again, so that she could never testify against him.

"Okay, I get it. I get why you wanted to return, and then disappear again. I can get an officer here as soon as I know you've landed in B.C. I can respect your decision, and do my best to get justice for Merri. Are you aware that she was murdered here at the bistro?"

The blood drained from her face. "I never made the connection," she said, her voice barely above a whisper. "I read that it had happened during a cooking lesson, but I assumed it took place at a cooking school." I tried to think back. It was true, the article about it had kindly not mentioned the bistro's name, though locals knew where it had occurred.

She practically ran to the window again to look out. I had purposely kept the lights dim so if anyone was watching from outside, they likely wouldn't be able to see anything in detail, especially since we were one floor up.

"Lexy, stop looking out the window. If by chance we are being watched, then I don't want anyone to get a good look at you. In any case, Giorgio has been out of town for a few days. Why are you so nervous? Has something happened that you're not telling me?"

"No, I'm probably just spooking myself. Maybe it's because of the unenthusiastic greeting I got from Georgie. She was always so nice to me, even after Giorgio started blackmailing Merri. I'm positive she never knew what her own brother was doing."

A thought occurred to me: "Lexy, are you aware that Georgie and Alan are now dating?"

"Alan and Georgie? That seems like an unlikely pair." She shook her head in amazement.

"Why did Merri come back, Lexy? Do you know?"

Her sudden smile lit up her face, before sadness washed over her again.

"She was coming to make peace with her family, tell them what had happened, and to finalize her divorce from Alan. You see, after I moved away Merri and I always stayed in touch. She eventually found the courage to find me, and we've been together ever since. We both lived quietly, but blissfully. She'd changed her name legally, don't ask me how but I'm sure she bribed someone–she did have powerful connections with whom she hadn't burned bridges."

She stood again and began to pace, like a lawyer making her summation.

"We dreamed of getting married and possibly adopting a child one day. Even though she'd changed her name, and there was no record of a previous marriage, it weighed on her conscience that she was still legally married. She wanted to do it right and prove her commitment to me, and for Alan's sake, so that he could have closure and be free to move forward with his life. She'd received every one of his emails and texts, imploring her for closure. As she got older, it weighed more heavily on her conscience."

"Did Alan know about this?"

"No, he didn't know it was her intention. She let him find out that she was here, and he insisted on papers being drawn up, at his expense. I strongly suspect he already had papers ready on the off chance that she ever showed up. She readily agreed to meet with him and his lawyer. In the meantime, her intention was to lay low, visit her family, and then sign the papers and slip away back to B.C. She hoped to be able to stay in touch with her family afterwards. Then Georgie somehow found out that she was here and insisted on a girls-night-out. Merri had told me she didn't know how to decline gracefully, and truthfully, I knew she missed Georgie. She certainly didn't know that she was dating Alan, I can tell you that much! If she had known, she would have thought twice about going out that night."

"You don't suppose Alan could have…" my question faltered. No, I had thought this one through plenty of times.

"Absolutely not," Lexy said without hesitation. "He had nothing to gain. He'd moved on with his life, so without a doubt, it was Giorgio, wanting to silence her forever and afraid that she'd turn him in, and certainly knowing that she would share her story with her family, given the chance. He couldn't take that chance."

My pseudo-aneurism twitched a few times. "Lexy, I seem to recall Georgie saying that she'd found out that Merri was here through Giorgio. Does that seem possible to you?"

"It seems ludicrous, but I wouldn't put it past her to call him or pay him a visit, just to indicate that he didn't intimidate her anymore. Maybe she even tried to blackmail him, now that he was the one with so much to lose. When she left Ottawa, she'd told him that she didn't care what he did anymore. So he did nothing. What could he do? She was already walking away from the life she had known with nothing."

"Nothing, except the money she swindled," I corrected, and she hung her head in consent.

At this point, it was nearing one in the morning. We'd gone through the half bottle of wine, as well as the majority of another that I'd opened. "You're not driving anywhere tonight, Lexy, I hope you know that. You can leave first thing in the morning after a strong cup of coffee and then I can take it from there. I'll show you to the cat room. Er, I mean, the guest room, if that's okay? I'm sure you're exhausted?"

"Yes, I'm drained and quite drunk, I might add. Thank you for that, it's numbed me a bit, which is rather nice, especially in light of the nature of our conversation." She brushed a quick tear aside as she followed me to the spare room.

Chapter Twenty-Five

I wish I could say that I fell asleep easily, but that wasn't the case. Of course I was weary to the bone, but realizing that I had forgotten to take my thyroid pill earlier that evening, I got out of bed around three in the morning. I usually took it in the evening since my body could apparently absorb the medicine better. Although I'd be fine if I missed it for one day, after a couple of days I would start to feel tired, which made me realize that I had also forgotten to take it the night before, since I was involved with Nathan at the time.

That thought triggered a train of other thoughts, none of which I needed to be considering since I'd already been tossing and turning and thinking about everything that Lexy had confided. And by four o'clock, I was so sleep deprived, and admittedly obsessed with Lexy, that I was beginning to question my own sexuality.

"This is ridiculous!" I grumbled to myself, losing all hope for sleep and turning on a light. Yes, Lexy was beautiful and captivating. Was it wrong to be so drawn to her? Or was it a normal reaction to some-one so stunning? I shifted gears and thought about Nathan. I felt my lips curl into a smile and my heart pitter-patter. Without a doubt, I loved him. In fact, when I thought about kissing Lexy on the lips, I could hear my inner voice saying "Nope!"

I also thought about the bistro, about my friends, my parents, about my tire that needed repair, and, yes, even my brother. That thought turned into thinking about siblings in general, Merri being Nathan's sibling, Georgie being Giorgio's. It was during this thought process that I finally gave up trying to sleep and got out of bed.

I found Lexy in the kitchen, staring bleakly at my coffee maker. "I don't know what to do," she said. "I don't know how to work it. I'm used to a Keurig." I brewed a pot while we both waited in silence at the kitchen counter. I was not a morning person, so the silence suited me fine. Only after we both had a half dozen sips did we attempt conversation.

"Did you get any sleep?" I mumbled politely.

"About two hours. How about you?"

"None. What time is your flight?"

"Nine."

It was now edging on six. "Do you have to return to a hotel room to check out or anything?" I asked, suddenly panicked.

"No. After meeting with you, I was just going to check in to the nearest hotel for the night, or maybe check in to the one closest to the airport, so I have everything that I brought with me in my rental car."

"Smart," I acknowledged. She had thought this through well. "Would you like some breakfast before you go?"

She shook her head. "Gosh, no. I can't eat this early. They'll be serving breakfast on the plane, anyway, so I'll be fine."

"Lexy, if you hadn't come here to tell me all this, what would you have done?"

"Maybe I would have written a letter, sent it to the police. I'm not quite sure. I wanted to approach Nathan's family, but they had moved some time during the last few years, and I couldn't track them down. I was so happy when he contacted me. I'm sorry, but I have to begin to get ready. If you wouldn't mind, would it be okay if I took a quick shower, changed my clothes?"

"By all means, go ahead."

With a crease on her otherwise flawless brow, she peered outside before unlocking the door and heading out to her car wearing the pyjamas I'd leant her the night before. Of course, she looked a million times better in them than I did, but I tried not to let that bother me. A super model I was not, but I am, normally, comfortable with my own looks.

She returned quickly with an overnight bag, relocked the door and headed to the bathroom. Fifteen minutes later, she emerged, fresh as a daisy while I still sat, slumped over my coffee. Yes, she was breathtaking, in hip-hugging jeans and a cute t-shirt, but I was relieved to note that I didn't feel like making out with her. I had done a lot of thinking during the night and had made some decisions that I only realized in that moment.

She felt my gaze and walked over to me. "Thank you, for everything. For listening, for the pjs, giving me a safe place to stay, and for everything that you'll be doing once I leave. Merri was a great person. You would have liked her." She leaned forward and put her arms around me in a fierce hug. Then, she quickly kissed me on the lips before breaking our embrace. Okay, maybe it wasn't super quick.

I gasped audibly, my hands flying to my lips. By then, she was already at the door. She turned and gave me a huge grin. "That's to help you decide." And then she was gone.

I rushed to the window and watched her get safely into her car and leave the parking lot. No one seemed to be following her, from what I could see from my limited vantage point. I returned to my coffee and jotted down my plan of action.

I would call Officer Lynette shortly after ten and ask if she could meet me at the bistro around five or six that evening. By then, Lexy would be safely back home and have had time to make herself *disappear*. Since that had been her plan all along, I could assume that everything was already in place for her to do so once her flight landed. I would tell Lynette everything that I knew and then she could handle it from there, since it was clearly out of my hands at this point. I didn't want to go anywhere near Giorgio and was happy that he'd been out of town the past few days.

Although I'd suspected he was involved, it was

entirely different knowing that he actually was the killer. It made my neck hairs rise to think I'd been in the same room with him.

It was still early, and since he'd worked the night shift, I knew that Nathan had probably gotten home and to sleep not long ago. I sent him a text to let him know that Lexy had visited me and that Giorgio was likely responsible for Merri's death. I would fill him in with all the details once he was awake and could contact me.

With nothing on my agenda for the next few hours, I decided to try out a new recipe for the bistro. I'd been thinking about introducing a cheese fondue recipe but had actually never tasted one myself. This seemed like the perfect time, if for no other reason than to distract myself until it was time to meet with Lynette.

By ten o'clock, I was on pins and needles and could wait no longer. I knew Lexy's plane was in the air by then, so I called Officer Lynette. Luckily, I got her machine. I love machines. I asked if she or another officer could swing by that evening and made a point of mentioning that I'd probably be out prior to then. I didn't want her coming by too early and risk jeopardizing Lexy's *disappearance* somehow.

Relieved once that part of the plan was executed, I got dressed, grabbed my purse and was about to head out the door to the cheese store. Out of habit, I glanced at the useless peephole and squawked when I saw it was covered with hair.

The hair knocked on the door, and all colour drained from my face.

Chapter Twenty-Six

"Hello? Are you okay in there?" Damn, she'd heard me yelp.

"Yes, yes! Just one minute," I called out. Think, think, think... Why was she here? What should I do? I spied my trusty bat, still on the floor near the couch. Okay, I had a weapon, just in case. I shook my head and laughed at myself. Get a grip. Was I afraid that Georgie would smother me to death with her hair?

Noting that I had forgotten to lock the door after Lexy had left, I grimaced. Even if I wasn't willing to open the door for her, she could have waltzed right in. As if she had read my mind, I saw the knob turn. I couldn't stall any longer and quickly launched the door open.

"Georgie! What a *pleasant* surprise! I'm sorry it took me so long, I was just getting dressed. " I stammered my fib as I plastered a smile onto my face and waited for her to explain her presence.

"Can you point me in the direction of your bathroom, please? I'm desperate after two coffees and being stuck in traffic." Open mouthed, I pointed down the hallway and she wiggled past me. My adrenaline quickly began to drop. I had been geared up for a confrontation, not a pee break.

A few minutes later, she joined me in the living room. I had moved my bat out of sight, yet still easily within reach. My instincts told me to be cautious, and I've learned the hard way to listen to them.

"May I offer you some coffee?" I hoped that she'd turn it down, but she didn't. No matter, I was giving her coffee that had been on the warmer for several hours. I practically scraped the sludge into a cup. "Sugar or cream?"

"Black, please." I gave her the mug of tar then sat at a safe distance from her.

"I have to admit that I'm startled by your visit," I managed to croak. "I hope you're not upset with me that I disturbed your supper hour."

"Hell, no. I just had some time to kill before meeting Giorgio for brunch, so I figured I'd stop by and say hello." She smiled, but it didn't seem genuine.

"Brunch?" My mind was spinning. The only place to have brunch around here was Leonardo's. "Where are you meeting for brunch?"

"Down the street," she answered vaguely. Did Leonardo even serve brunch?

I lost patience. "Georgie, why are you really here? Is there some way I can help you?"

She put down her mug and tapped her perfectly manicured fingernails on my coffee table. The rhythm of her tapping almost hypnotized me, until a shock of realization electrified my body.

Of course, she was in the salon industry, hence she'd have easy access to manicures. She'd previously mentioned being on her feet all day, cutting hair. Nothing wrong with that, my inner voice confirmed. No, however, what was wrong was that her house didn't fit her profession. She didn't have quite the fancy, expensive house that her brother had, but the area she lived in was pricey, and it was a good-sized, two-story, house. It was certainly out of the price range of a hair stylist. So where did she get the money to purchase such a house?

This inner conversation took place in the matter of seconds, but I was sure that Georgie could see the light bulb turn on above my head.

"Well, I'm glad you could stop by. I was just on my way out, to go shopping with a friend, so I can only spare another moment or two. And I'm sure you don't want to be late for your breakfast with Giorgio," I babbled as I stood, hoping she'd follow suit and follow me to the door, and also hoping that I was wrong about everything. I inched my way forward, afraid to turn my back on her.

Not only did she not follow me, she wriggled comfortably on my couch and put her feet up onto the coffee table. "Giorgio said he'd meet me here, actually. Isn't that nice? Oh, did Lexy make it safely onto her plane?"

And there we had it. The cards were now on the table.

My heart dropped into my stomach. "As far as I

know… Did she mention that she was leaving today when you saw her yesterday?"

"Yes, she did. I went online to check what flights were leaving for B.C. today. There weren't any. I waited there, as of six this morning, to make sure she was leaving town for good. Luckily for her, she showed up, and then boarded a flight to Chicago. Interesting choice… That's a huge airport; I'm sure she will connect with another flight there. I'm not too concerned; it's clear that she intends to disappear, which is fine by us. For now, anyway… Now you, on the other hand…"

She let the sentence dangle in mid-air. Basically, she was telling me that she and Giorgio were about to *make me disappear*.

"Me? Like I said, I'm disappearing right now to go shopping. Which reminds me, I haven't done my hair or makeup yet. If you'll excuse me…" I made a move toward the washroom so that I could try to call 911 or text someone for help, but she stopped me in my tracks.

"You're not going anywhere. Sit here while we wait for Giorgio." She motioned toward the couch.

"I don't think I want to see Giorgio," I mumbled as I sat dutifully where she pointed. The bat that I had hidden just underneath the sofa brushed reassuringly against the back of my foot, giving me a glimmer of hope and a spark of courage.

"Then let's have another cup of coffee and try to get to know each other a little better," I suggested, hoping to distract her. Hairdressers usually liked to chat and divulge all sorts of information. I had to try to use this time to my advantage while I waited for just the right moment to strike.

"I'll pour you one just to shut you up," she retorted. She walked over to the pot, glancing over her shoulder to keep an eye on me, preventing me from making my move.

The remaining sludge from the coffee pot oozed slowly into the cup. She glanced down at it in disgust and I quickly bent down, extending my hand under the couch. As my fingers fumbled, they succeeded in pushing the bat out of my reach. *Bazd meg!* I quickly focused my attention on my foot, pretending I was adjusting my sock, before she caught me fumbling. I could not risk having her discover the bat.

"Are you really going to drink this?" she asked as she placed the cup at the far end of the coffee table.

"I like it strong," I fibbed, thinking fast. Maybe I could use that as a weapon. I shimmied down the couch, neither of us taking our eyes off the other. She remained standing a few feet away.

My hands firmly on the cup, I held it casually on my lap, though my body was coiled for action. I took a deep breath. "Why, Georgie? She was your best friend."

Her eyes hardened as she let loose a strangled garble of a laugh.

"Why? Why not, I ask in return. She 'borrowed' money from me, too, you know. I know I told you she didn't, but she did. I loaned her almost everything I had, and back then, I didn't have much. She took me for a fool, like she did everyone else, so all those years of friendship obviously meant nothing."

"Is that why you came to the bistro with her that night, hoping to talk to her about paying you back?"

She laughed genuinely this time. "You still haven't quite figured it all out, have you? No matter, you know too much. Giorgio will know what to do with you." She admired her manicured claws. Yes, let's not get any blood on them, shall we?

The realization hit me then, the true extent of her involvement. "You lured her to my bistro. It was all pre-planned, wasn't it? You weren't just involved in helping Giorgio blackmail her, you helped to set up her murder! But why here with so many people around?"

This time she frowned. "I actually had nothing to do with blackmailing her. That was all Giorgio's doing. But then I found out, so my dear brother had no choice but to share the money with me. Giorgio was never good with money and was too dumb to open his own business, so I knew something was going on. When Merri left town and everyone started coming forward about having been ripped off by her, I had a hunch and confronted Giorgio. He was so proud of himself and bragged about having blackmailed her for money and forcing her to provide free legal services to help him open up his business. By the time I figured it out, his business was doing surprisingly well and he set me up with my beautiful house to keep me quiet."

"I thought you weren't close."

"We aren't. But we're still family."

"So what about the night she was killed?" I prompted as I got ready to strike.

"Yes, that was an unfortunate turn of events, her showing up after all these years. Would you believe she visited Giorgio and tried to blackmail him by threatening to turn him in? He agreed to give her some money, pretending he'd need a couple of days to make arrangements. She fell for his ruse, and of course those arrangements involved getting rid of her. Who better to help but family?" She paused and shrugged.

"Hey, I could use the money he was offering me for my help, and it's not like she even bothered to call me to say hello or apologize," she continued. "So I called her, pretending to want to see her, and suggested this place. I liked the idea of a wine tasting and figured getting her tipsy would make things easier. It would certainly make it more pleasant for me. Plus the location was great, being right next to that stretch of forest. I made sure I parked as close to that part of the lot as possible. The initial plan was that I was suddenly going to get a migraine and ask that we leave a bit early; just early enough that no one would be out there but us. Giorgio would be lying in wait and then attack her in the parking lot before we reached my car and then push me down and 'steal' my purse to make it look good."

"So, what happened to change that?" I prompted her. She was almost agitated enough to be taken off guard. If I could just keep her talking… My grip tightened on the cup of molten lava.

"Giorgio was growing impatient and kept texting me for updates. I could tell that Merri was getting suspicious, with my phone lighting up all the time, so I was starting to feel jumpy and decided to leave earlier than planned. As she headed to the bathroom, I texted Giorgio that we'd soon be leaving. What I didn't know then was that he'd been right out in front, looking inside, and saw her head to the bathroom. No one else was around, so he came inside and waited for her in that dimly lit area. When she opened the door, he bashed her in the head from behind with one of those massive candles you keep on all the tables. I guess he got her just in the right spot because the blow knocked her out. He caught her before she hit the ground, dragged her back into the bathroom and closed the door. She was still breathing so he said he just kept hitting her with the candle until he was sure she couldn't be saved."

Lost in the memory, she let her guard down and I jumped at my chance. I threw the coffee in her face even though by now it had lost its heat. It was just enough of a distraction for me to push the couch back with my foot and grab the bat. As I was still bent over, she jumped on my back before I could turn around and sent me sprawling onto the floor. She managed to snake an arm around my neck and I could feel the squeeze against my already deficient thyroid area. I bucked my head back, making contact with her face.

She screamed in pain, her hands flying to her face to protect it from further damage as she scrambled to her feet. My hands now firmly on the bat, I lunged after her, managing to barely strike her across one knee. As I prepared to strike again, she charged me and managed to deflect my blow with her arm before knocking me backward. I stumbled, but my grip held firm.

Quickly regaining my footing, I rushed at her, this time striking her in the head, and again, across the knees. I kept striking, and screaming, and striking and screaming, even as she lay motionless on the ground, and still kept striking when I heard my door crash open.

Suspecting that it was Giorgio, I aimed in the direction of the door and charged blindly, still screaming, as I crashed right into my brother. Recognition set in only once I'd landed a good blow to his shoulder.

"Sorry!" I screamed, "Someone's coming to kill me!" Stephen stood, rooted in the same spot, unable to take in what was happening quickly enough to respond other than to grab his shoulder in pain. A figure loomed in the doorway behind him as I screamed again. "Watch out!" Once again, I charged. He screamed, I screamed...

And Officer Lynette screamed.

"Omff!" she exhaled as I clipped her on the arm. Her reflexes were quick, though, and she quickly disabled me. "What's going on, Amalia?" she shouted as she threw my bat to the ground and put me in an arm-lock.

She was referring to the mess I'd made of Georgie, my screaming, and the message that I had left for her earlier. Pointing at Georgie, I tried to reply as calmly as possible, my voice still shrill. "She's also responsible for Merri's death, and her brother, Giorgio, is going to try to kill me."

Her steely gaze fell on my brother and his eyes grew wide. "No! That's not him. This is my brother, remember?" Recognition sparked in her eyes, remembering him from the day of the break-in.

She let go of me slowly. "Relax, Amalia. I have everything under control. If he's in the area, he'll see my police cruiser and steer clear. Now, you sit as quietly as you can while I get some backup to watch for him and get this woman an ambulance."

Chapter Twenty-Seven

Hours later, my brother and I sat in stunned silence. Georgia had groaned as Officer Lynette cuffed her and before the ambulance attendants took her away. I was relieved that I hadn't killed her and wondered if she would have killed me. She seemed to have wanted to leave that task up to Giorgio, who, luckily for me, had not shown up on time.

We later learned that he'd been delayed by traffic, the same traffic that Georgie had mentioned when she showed up at my door. I sent up a silent prayer to the traffic gods of Ottawa and vowed never to curse rush hour again.

We could only speculate as to why Merri would visit and threaten Giorgio after all this time. I suspected that she felt empowered, being back in town, tying up loose ends, being in love, having rebuilt her life and hoping to make amends with family. She likely figured Giorgio deserved to squirm a little, which, of course, he did, but she had underestimated him.

I looked over at Stephen, who was staring blankly

into his wine glass. "So, what brings you by?" I joked feebly. He just shook his head.

"I came by to let you know I'm heading back to Montreal. Amalia, you're going to give our parents a heart attack if this keeps up!"

I bristled. "Do you think any of this was intentional? All I want is a nice, quiet life, eating cheese and salami, and drinking wine. I didn't ask for any of this to happen. What about you? Your actions just about broke up the family. Mom wouldn't even talk to me or to dad, so you have a lot of nerve."

He rushed to explain. "I'm just trying to process everything that has happened." He tugged at his goatee then scratched at his itchy eyes as the cats snuggled closer to him. I snickered to myself. He deserved to suffer, a little.

His shoulders sagged further as he let out a big sigh. "You were right. I was laid off at work. I still have the other job, but it doesn't pay very well, and I got carried away again with gambling. I'm going to get professional help to overcome that, as soon as I get home. I swear on your moustache," he said in all seriousness.

As always, I forgave him. We didn't talk about the break-in. It didn't matter, at this point. After another hour and another glass of wine, he said goodbye and headed to my parents' place for his final night in Ottawa.

It was well past midnight when I picked up the phone to call Nathan. Yes, I called, as in actually spoke on the phone with him, something we never did. I, in particular, hated speaking on a phone, so all we ever did was text.

He answered on the third ring, panicked. "Is that really you or did you butt-dial me by accident? Are you okay? Why are you calling?"

I hesitated, just a heartbeat. My pseudo-aneurism pulsed. But when I spoke, a sense of calm washed over me.

"It's time to reinvent myself. I'm moving in with you."

Swiss Cheese Fondue

- 1 tablespoon butter
- 1 teaspoon or slightly more cornstarch or flour
- 1 cup milk
- 1/4 teaspoon salt, dash of paprika and sprinkling of dill
- 1 cup shredded Swiss (such as Emmental) and 1 cup shredded other cheese of choice (ex; pre-shredded bags like Tex-Mex, or a lovely brie)
- Salt and pepper to taste. A dash of garlic powder is also good.

Melt butter over medium heat and add cornstarch or flour, cooking for a minute or so. Pour the milk into this mixture and stir with a whisk until slightly bubbling then turn heat down to a simmer. Continue stirring until a bit thickened, a minute or two then add cheeses and stir until blended and melted.

If using a fondue pot, keep on lowest heat setting (if it has heat settings). If using a saucepan on the stove, remove from stove once everything melts and is combined.

Some ideas of what to dip in the fondue:

Bread chunks (pumpernickle, sour dough, french), pita or corn chips, cubed ham chunks or cooked sausage chunks, cubed cooked potatoes, broccoli, cauliflower, fresh mushrooms.

Enjoy while warm and melty.

Epilogue

A lot has happened during the Whine & Cheese quadrilogy. Are you curious about how things worked out over the years?

First off, let's set the record straight. While Amalia's quirky personality and some life events were based loosely on me (Judy), I do not own any yellow underwear and push up bras. *You can all stop envisioning me in those. Please!*

Georgie and Giorgio are in jail, of course.

I briefly felt sad for Alan, his girlfriend having played a role in the death of his estranged wife, but he ended up dating Sherri again, as you must have guessed.

Lexy contacted Nathan via email years later to say that she was well and safe. She never divulged any further details.

Nicole and Drew are still dating and contemplating moving in together. Unfortunately, Nicole is a neat freak and isn't sure she wants to be cleaning up after someone else.

Nora and her husband, Craig, are still attending

couples counselling. During one session, he let it slip that he thought she drank too much wine. Well, she got up and walked out. He hasn't said a word since and she's gone on to become a Sommelier.

Billy continues to do well on his medication and enrolled in culinary school. Chloé is taking business courses. They've been flirting and getting close, but Billy hasn't quite mustered the nerve to ask her out…yet.

Hans and his model girlfriend moved to Toronto, however, the stress of the move, combined with the pressures of being a model, sent her into a depression. She used food to comfort herself, which ended up being a blessing in disguise. She is now a lot healthier than she was and has successfully become a full-fig-ured model. Meanwhile, Hans took a job as a men's clothing salesperson. He enjoys the employee dis-count and continues to build his wardrobe.

Amalia's group of friends run the bistro and share the profits equally.

Amalia and Stella went on to be close friends, despite the fact that she got pregnant by Officer Sean. Surprisingly, he was elated by the news and asked her to marry him. She declined…for now. Just to be clear, we're talking about Stella here.

Stephen is working two jobs again, trying to pay down his gambling debts. He has kept his word and continues to get counselling for gambling addiction.

Mr. Kis is now a yogi. As it turns out, he really enjoyed those classes that Mrs. Kis dragged him to. Despite his bad knee, he does a wicked Tree Pose and often wears flowy, white pants. Luckily, not in public.

Mrs. Kis was finally able to enroll in Polish dancing classes and reenrolled so many times that they finally asked her to teach the next one. She's lost forty pounds and looks amazing. She still wears her t-shirts from the bistro with boldly coloured sweat pants.

Mrs. Knuedle and Milton? Still going strong! They both retired and moved to Florida where Amalia often visits them.

Mr. Leonardo was shrewd enough to invest heavily in the company that made his favourite brand of pepperoni. He made a fortune and sold the pizza place. Unfortunately, he too moved to Florida, and Amalia had the misfortune of running into him at a Papa John's, while visiting Mrs. Knuedle and Milton. Imagine the look on their faces!

After the last fiasco at the bistro, Amalia did indeed decide to move to Kingston to be with Nathan. While she still owns the bistro, she's seldom there. She does visit and helps out from time to time, just for old time's sake. She rents out the upstairs living quarters to Officer Sean and Stella and actually makes a profit. The second bedroom, formerly the cat room, is now a cute, frilly, pink baby room. Not surprisingly, there have been no further crimes at the bistro.

The former owners, Harold and Harriet, have expressed an interest in buying back the bistro, but Amalia has rejected their offer for now.

Hummer, sweet Hummer, passed away many years later. He had a happy life and is dearly missed. Bart is all grown up now and looks like a mini panther. He likes to sleep in boxes or on Amalia's feet.

Nathan was offered a permanent position in Kingston as an emergency services team leader.

And Amalia *is still in the process of reinventing herself.*

For the last time,
Cheers, my friends!